Camp Green Forest

A. A. Johnson

Dedicated above all to Jesus, the truest friend anyone can have, and then to my best friend Katie. I can't imagine my life without either of you!

Although she grew up on her family's Christian campground, Sammi spent her life running from the only arms that could hold her together through the toughest storms of life.

Chapter 1

"California?! Why?! Sammi, there's nothing for you out there except trouble. The best place for you is right here, running the family camp. Your mother and I always prayed before you were born that God would give you the desire to serve Him here."

"You prayed?! Oh! What a lotta good that did! Look at how God answered those prayers, by taking my mother away when I was so tiny and leaving you to raise me on your own. Why would I want to serve a god like that?"

"Sammi, don't talk like that," her father pleaded. "God loves you more than you could ever imagine. You just have to…"

"No! I don't have to do anything! How can you stand there and tell me God loves me? What do you even know about me? You were too busy running this place to notice that I wanted no part of your God! California is where the best ad exec jobs are, and that's where I'm going! I've already gotten my college acceptance. Besides I'm eighteen now, so you really have no say in this. I'm going to live the life I want! I can't wait to get away from this middle-of-nowhere, empty hole!" Sammi was nearly screaming with disgust. How could her father not recognize her advertising talent and support her desires for her own life? Why did he insist on trying to force her to run the family summer camp? She could never believe in a God that would leave a tiny baby with no mother!

Justin couldn't believe that his worst fears were coming true. He could feel tears beginning to flood his eyes. Why couldn't his only child, his precious daughter, see that he only wanted what was best for her? He prayed and prayed throughout Sammi's life that she would believe in God's love and understand that He has reasons for allowing bad things to happen that could not be comprehended by mere humans. Justin was sure she would drift farther away from the truth if she moved to California. Why was God taking so long to answer his prayers for his daughter? He continued to pray that she would experience God's love for her before it was too late.

"Oh, Sammi. I wish you could see how much God loves you. It's not about what you feel He might have "taken" from you, but about what He offers you through His Son."

"Please, Dad! Don't start preaching at me again. I don't believe and don't want to hear it! Don't you think it's about time *you* believe in *me*?"

"I do believe in you, Sammi! I know you are a very talented girl, but I believe God wants so much more for you..."

"No! Dad, just stop it! I told you I am not going to listen to this again! If God wants so much more for me, then He should have let me grow up with a mother to love me and teach me all the things I've missed. I don't believe it! I won't listen another minute! I'm going to California, and I'm not coming back! You have pushed me too far with all your preaching! Sorry I'm such a disappointment to you for not believing in your God who leaves little girls without mothers!"

With that, Sammi stormed out, letting the door slam behind her, as her father called after her, while tears began streaming down his cheeks.

Justin fell to his knees and prayed as he had so many times before, "Lord, I will never give up on my daughter, and I know that You will not either. Please reach out to her and help her to understand Your love for her. And my love for her as well. Father, she's so lost. I pray You will bring her back to us."

Driving around the bend, Sammi was not prepared for the desolate sight that greeted her. She knew her father had been ill and having difficulty caring for the campgrounds, but the rundown state of the camp was quite shocking. Who knew eighteen years away from home would change things so much?

As she sat staring out the windshield, she reflected back all those years ago to the days of summer fun. "This place brings back a lot of old memories," she thought. "Candace and I always had so much fun. Those were good times. Camp wasn't all bad. If only Dad wasn't always so disappointed in me. I just couldn't believe in God like he wanted me to. Is that really such a bad thing? I can think of so many worse things that children do to disappoint their parents." Sammi had been angry for a very long time. This place brought up the anger in a way she was unprepared for. She wanted to lash out about so many things that she hadn't even thought about in years.

"No, I don't have time to dwell on these disappointments! There's too much to do here. I need to face what is in front of me, get this done, and get back to California. The sooner the better."

Chapter 2

The gate was rusty and falling off its hinges; halfway open, it blocked the left side of the road. The wrought iron sign arching over the gate once read "Camp Green Forest," but over the past few years, vandals had broken off several letters and pieces, leaving only partial letters that no longer spelled anything. The dry and dusty dirt road was deserted and lonely except for the three stray mutts that were roaming around, searching for their next meal.

A small grey squirrel crept up next to the grass at the edge of the road and paused, looking around for more acorns to stuff in its cheeks. The largest of the dogs caught the scent of the squirrel first and began to bark. The squirrel froze with fear for an instant, and then, realizing the imminent danger, sprinted back into the undergrowth. The three dogs were close behind, but not close enough as the squirrel scampered up a nearby tree. Each dog barked and leapt up the trunk of the tree for several minutes before deciding it was a lost cause and meandering back toward the road in search of other prey.

Forty years ago, this place was overrun not with weeds but with teenagers. The site's ten cabins housed two hundred campers and twenty counselors. As word of mouth spread about how much fun each camper had at Camp Green Forest, more and more teens wanted to attend. Every year there were at least another thirty-five teens on the waiting list for camp. But looking at it now, Sammi knew Grandpa Gerald would come unglued if he was around to witness the disarray of his old campground.

Justin Alexander's family had owned Camp Green Forest since the early 1950's. It had been a big tradition for children to spend their summers there, not only teens from Chase County, but from the surrounding counties as well. Justin's grandfather had the vision to begin building the camp in 1952 with only two cabins (one for boys and one for girls), and he insisted on establishing it on Christian values. Not only could the children learn various arts, crafts, and sports, but most importantly, Gerald Alexander wanted to provide them with the opportunity to know God. He provided a curriculum to enable them "grow in grace and in the knowledge of their Lord and Savior" as the apostle Peter had written in his letter. To be sure that the Gospel was heard by all, campers were required to attend worship service every evening where the camp preacher would share the Gospel, and additional Bible study classes were offered in the morning as an alternative to the arts, crafts, and sports.

Justin's father, Gregory, followed in Gerald's footsteps, as did Justin. Each man worked hard to maintain the grounds and make the necessary repairs every year. Through the years, cabins were added (always two at a time, something Grandpa Gerald referred to as Noah's way). When Justin became the director, he often wished they had more land on which to continue building cabins, but he refused to build on the sports fields that attracted so many campers or lose the woods that helped to keep the camp secluded. Hundreds upon hundreds of children had decided to receive and follow Christ through the years at Camp Green Forest. Thousands, possibly, but not the one Justin most desired would decide to follow.

Justin spent thirty-seven and a half years as camp director. Of course, he had helped his father and grandfather for many years before becoming the director himself. In the 1980s, it was still a booming and growing business, but by 2010, it seemed that most children had lost interest in attending camps, and parents no longer wanted to send their children. Justin blamed technology. Teens would much rather spend their summers with their noses buried in cell phones and other devices, and parents spent more money on the latest high-tech gadgets rather than paying for camp.

Now the weeds were growing up and overtaking the buildings. The roofs were leaky, and several windows were broken in each cabin. Shutters were hanging loose and crooked. Most of the benches in the main hall/tabernacle were broken and rotting. A tree had fallen into the main area of the cafeteria, and a family of raccoons had made the kitchen their home. Down by the lake, eight of the thirty canoes were busted and scattered among the cattails that had taken over the shore line. The dock was beginning to sink farther and farther into the murky water of the lake.

Five years ago, Justin had been forced to resign as caretaker and director of the camp when his doctor discovered Justin's heart was extremely enlarged and about to give out from the strain of working harder than normal to pump his blood. Justin had hoped his only child would come home to save the camp and become the next director, but she had been in Europe at the time and made it explicitly clear that she had no desire to set foot in Green Forest again and definitely would not run the camp. She had cut her ties with the family years before and wanted nothing to do with their "religion" or their rules that she felt denied her the pleasures in life she sought. Still, Justin continued to pray for her daily and never gave up hope that one day his prodigal would return.

It had been years since Justin saw Sammi. She was eighteen then, out of high school and leaving for college. He could never forget the day she left. She was so upset, thinking that he didn't believe in her, but all he ever wanted was for her to believe in God as he did. He had hoped and often prayed she'd come home before his time on earth was over, but she would not even call. Was it possible that his enlarged heart could feel any emptier?

If only her mother had been here to help me raise her, he thought. *Maybe she could have made a difference. Sammi always questioned why You took her mother from her, God. I did the best I could to explain, but it never seemed to be enough.* He prayed, *Lord, I know You can still bring her home to me and to You. I pray Your will be done. Amen.*

Justin and Crystal had met at the camp when she volunteered to be the pianist for the summer of 1978. She was a brilliant player, and he could tell that her music came from a heart full of love for her Savior. They quickly became inseparable, and held a wedding ceremony in the midst of the falling, golden autumn leaves at the camp that November.

Crystal wanted a large family, and was soon expecting their first child. The pregnancy ended in a miscarriage, but Crystal's faith was strong and the couple tried again and again to conceive. After nearly three years, they had almost given up when she became pregnant for the second time, they were overjoyed. It was an extremely difficult pregnancy, but Crystal was able to carry the baby to term in spite of the many complications. The effects were devastating on Crystal, however, and there wasn't much hope for the large family she wanted to bear. The baby was healthy from birth, but despite all the doctor's efforts, Crystal never fully recovered. For the following twenty-three weeks and five days, Crystal loved little Sammi more than toast loves butter.

That was their saying. *More than toast loves butter.* Justin remembered the first time Crystal said it shortly after they were married. They had been testing cliches to choose one of their own but with a personal twist. When Crystal was fixing breakfast one morning, she said, "I love you more than toast loves butter," and Justin knew that would be their saying forever. He could still hear her saying it every time he ate toast, and it always made him smile and wipe a tear from his eye.

Oh, Crystal, if only you'd had more time with us. If only Sammi could have known how much you loved her. Mom and Angie did the best they could as stand-in mother figures, but I know it just wasn't the same as having you here would have been.

Chapter 3

Standing on the campgrounds all these years later, Sammi could barely believe her eyes. *Has it really only been five years since Dad had to resign as camp manager? How could this place become such a dump so quickly? Dad and Grandpa always worked so hard every year to make sure this place stood up to its reputation as the best camp in Chase County. Now look at it!* she thought.

In the late 80s and early 90s, it was the most entertaining place for a teenager to spend the summer. She always had so much fun playing sports, swimming, canoeing, and hiking in the woods. She loved adventure, but she never cared for the religious lessons they had to listen to everyday. She would doodle and daydream through the required sermons in the evening and never opted for the additional classes offered in the mornings. For Sammi, the best part of camp had to be making new friends and reuniting with old friends each summer. Through the years, she had made dozens of close friends, but there was one friend who meant the world to Sammi.

Candace, her best friend who was more like the big sister she never had, was always there for Sammi, no matter what life held for them. They met when Sammi was eight; Candace was nine, but only six months older. Candace and her family moved into the small farmhouse a quarter mile down the road. The two young girls soon had a path worn between their houses. Because their birthdays were so close, they were in the same class in school.

They were inseparable, always playing outside, exploring the woods and naming different areas, having picnics, running away from Candace's mean pet goose, or playing house inside on rainy days.

"Hey, Sammi!" Candace called across her yard as Sammi came walking up.

"Hi, Candace! What do you want to do today?"

"Why don't we pack a lunch and walk down to 'Flowerland' at the bottom of the hill and have a picnic?"

"Sounds great! Will your mom mind if we make some pb&j sandwiches and take some Hostess cupcakes? I love the way she keeps them cool in the fridge!"

"I'm sure she won't care, but let's go ask."

"Don't forget the Cheetos!"

"You got it! Hey, Mom..."

Then off the girls would go to explore, picnic in hand, being goofy and giggling. They would make up silly songs and sing them in funny accents as they splashed through the mud puddles the rain had left earlier that morning, laughing at their own silliness. "Splish, splash *go the footsies as we're walking down the road." They enjoyed spending the day roaming through the woods, looking for treasure, splashing in the little brook that flowed between their properties, making flower bracelets, climbing trees, and reclining in lawn chairs searching for pictures in the clouds. In the evening, they would often sit by the fire pit, eating seedless green grapes and gazing at the stars.*

Sammi often reminded Candace of how lucky she was to have such a wonderful mother like Angie. "Your mom is the coolest, Candace. I wish..."

"Sammi, you know Mom loves you as much as she loves me, well almost, anyway. I know you miss your own mother and even though your grandma does the best she can, it's not the same. But you're still very lucky, because your dad loves you way more than my parents love me. At least I feel that way sometimes. Mom can get so grumpy when she's tired from working and the house is a mess. You just never see her that way."

"You may be right. I know my dad loves me, probably more than most parents. Sometimes it's too much. He can be so protective that it feels like he's smothering me with love."

"Oh, Sammi, you know that's just another way he shows his love for you. But whenever you need to get away, just remember I'm right down the road, and you are part of this family too. Mom always calls you my 'sister from another mister.'"

At that, both girls would laugh and hug each

other.

They knew they would be the best of friends forever.

     As they grew up, they shared all their secrets and most of their clothes too, just like sisters. There were only two things they never shared: boys (naturally) and religion. Candace was a strong believer and follower of Christ, but she knew that Sammi wasn't interested in being a Christian. Candace never let that stop her from loving Sammi or from praying for her though. Candace believed some day Sammi would realize her need for Christ's forgiveness and accept Him. Candace had to believe Sammi would one day change her ways before it was too late.

Chapter 4

Sammi never bought into the beliefs of her family, no matter how much her father had tried to convince her. Why couldn't he understand that the Christian life was fine for him, but not for her. She thought it was just nonsense; she was happy living her life the way she wanted.

She had been around the world and seen and done many wonderful things. She had been serenaded while floating in a gondola in the canals of Venice, had eaten filet mignon in a restaurant at the top of the Eiffel Tower, had toured the castles of Ireland, had seen a lion up close on safari in Africa, had swum along the Great Barrier Reef, had watched kangaroos jump across the Outback, and had had countless other adventures around the world.

Sammi also had had several "loves" in her lifetime and had learned something about people from each one. The main thing she had learned was that, even though someone said he loved her, no one truly did. She had nearly married one, the best love of her life, Dusty Newall. He had always been so kind to her, yet she often felt like there was a distance between them. She could still remember when they first met. Of course, it had been at Camp Green Forest.

When Sammi was thirteen, she was finally able to attend camp as a camper for the first time. She was nervous but excited. As the director's daughter, she had spent every summer there and knew all about the camp, but this year she would not be just the director's daughter; she would be a camper. She did not want any special treatments, and she wanted to stay in a camper cabin, not the director's cabin. Justin didn't necessarily like the idea, but he knew what it was like. He had enjoyed being the director's son when he first started attending as a camper, but some of the other children had given him a hard time about it. He agreed it would be better for her and let her stay in the first year cabin with the other girls.

Dusty arrived at the camp a day early with his mom who served as the head cook in the camp cafeteria that year. Sammi and Dusty did not hit it off immediately. In fact, Sammi didn't much care for him the first few weeks of camp. Even at thirteen, she'd decided she wasn't interested in those goody-goody Christian boys.

Over the summer though, as Dusty, Candace, and Sammi had to compete on the same team and sit through the same classes, the three of them began to become good friends. They spent much of their free time talking to each other and walking around the campgrounds. Candace could tell that Dusty was starting to really like Sammi, but she also knew her best friend well enough to know that Sammi wasn't feeling the same about him.

"Sammi, why don't you give Dusty a chance? I mean as more than a friend. He clearly likes you and wants to be more than friends."

"Oh, I don't know, Candace," Sammi responded flippantly, rolling her eyes.

"He's so sweet and totally handsome. Did you see him carrying that canoe the other day? Wow!"

"No doubt about it; he's built! I didn't think you would be checking him out though. Isn't that against the rules?" Sammi teased.

"Well...I am human, you know. Dusty's mom really seems to like you too. So what's the problem? Why aren't you falling for him?" Candace questioned.

"I guess he's just too involved with all this religious stuff. You know how I feel about Dad pressuring me about it all the time. The last thing I need is a boyfriend doing the same."

"Sammi, I hope you realize soon that 'this religious stuff' is not nearly as bad as you think. Remember I used to think it was silly too, but the more that I read the Bible, the more real it became. Now I can't imagine my life without it."

"That's fine for you, Can, but I just don't want any part of it myself. Hey! Isn't it time for the big competition down at the volleyball court? Come on! We don't want to miss that!" With that, Sammi hopped off the deck of their cabin and began running toward the volleyball court.

"Okay, fine, change the subject," Candace called after her. *That's what you always do, but I'm not through praying for you to accept the Lord as your Savior*, she thought. Then she chased after Sammi hollering, "Sammi, slow down! Wait for me!"

Their team won the tournament and the three friends celebrated by convincing Dusty's mom to let them have a banana split party. It was a great day.

As the summer came to an end, Sammi realized that she would truly miss Dusty. They promised to write to each other every week. Candace overheard them exchanging addresses, and with a smug smile, she thought, *Finally, my prayers are starting to affect her. Thank You, Lord!*

Sammi and Dusty kept in contact for a few years, just as friends. Each summer, the *Tres Amigos* (Sammi, Dusty, and Candace) would reunite at Camp Green Forest. Candace began to call Dusty her brother from another mother; she really admired him for his spiritual strength. He began to be more involved in Bible study and even encouraged the girls to join him for extra devotional times. Sammi cherished his friendship, but always reminded him that she wasn't into all that. He never pressured her about it, and she would go off to watch a baseball game or go swimming while Dusty and Candace had Bible study. The two spent most of their time praying for Sammi, and encouraging each other not to give up on her.

When Sammi was seventeen, Dusty and his mother Hannah moved to town. Hannah was tired of the big city life since their neighborhood had become so rough. "This is the only place I've ever been that I truly feel God is near me," she told Justin. "Every year, I look forward to coming back and cooking at the camp so much that it's like my own little piece of heaven on earth."

"The camp hasn't had a better cook since my own mother was in charge of the kitchen. It's great to have you living so near," Justin replied.

The girls were happy that the Tres Amigos wouldn't have to wait for summer to reunite, and the trio soon became a regular sight at Dominique's Pizza Palace in town every Friday. On Sundays, they took turns going to each other's houses after church to eat lunch and spend the afternoon together.

By the time they were eighteen, Dusty and Sammi admitted that they cared for each other as more than friends and decided to give dating a try. Sammi and Dusty's first few weeks together as a couple were the best time she'd ever had. They soon realized that they shared many interests and likes. One of these was a love for the beach. In fact, that's the reason they started dating. There weren't any beaches around Camp Green Forest, but Sammi often expressed her dream to go to California and live near the beach. Dusty would tell her that he couldn't think of anything better than to live in a beach house, so for her eighteenth birthday, he gave her a small, aqua bottle with a cork in the top and some brown twine tied in a bow around the bottle's neck. Inside the bottle was just a little bit of sand and a tiny, plastic, two-story house. He said he knew how much she wanted a beach house, and the gesture touched her so deeply that she agreed to date him.

They were so in love, or at least she thought they were. As they began to get really serious about each other, however, the arguments began and continued to get worse. She wanted him and he admitted that he wanted her too, but he insisted on waiting, on "doing it the right way." He wanted to be married first. He said he couldn't marry her though if she would not "become a Christian." That was the last thing in the world that Sammi wanted to do, and eventually they decided it would never work between them and went their separate ways.

Sammi was forced to question if she would ever be able to trust anyone.

But that was all so long ago, and who knows where Dusty is now? He didn't even keep in touch with Candace. Oh well. Sammi forced herself to leave her musings of the past and get back to work on her ad campaign.

Chapter 5

After high school, Sammi left to attend college in California, while Candace married Jimmy, whom she had met at camp the year before, and began raising a family. The girls kept in touch, talking on the phone for hours at least once a week, but they rarely saw each other, with Candace busy with the kids' activities and Sammi traveling around all the time. Even though they weren't close in proximity, they were always close at heart. Sammi loved Candace's children, Canaan and Cady, as if they were her own children and was constantly sending them gifts from her latest trip.

The last time they saw each other face-to-face was when Candace and Jimmy brought the kids out to California for Christmas six years earlier. Canaan was eight and Cady was six. It was quite an experience for Sammi; she wasn't accustomed to having children in the house, let alone children overly excited with the anticipation of opening Christmas presents. She had spent a lot of money on their gifts and was excited as well, hoping they would love what she had gotten them. Before they opened their gifts, Jimmy brought out his Bible and read from the gospel of Luke about the first Christmas. He reminded his children about the true meaning of the holiday and that Jesus was the best gift they could ever receive. Sammi smiled but rolled her eyes.

Later, as she and Candace were sitting on the patio catching up on the latest news from each other's lives, Candace brought up the subject. "Thank you for giving such wonderful gifts to the kids. Canaan loves the ThinkPad, and Cady has been wanting a doll like that for months. It's amazing how well you know them even though you don't get to see them much."

"It's my pleasure to spoil them for you. I do wish we could get together more often," Sammi replied.

"Well, you know, your dad would love for you to move back home and help him with the camp. Now that Jimmy and I have bought my parents' old place, we would be so close, just like old times."

"Not gonna happen, Can. You know I love you, but I can't deal with Dad pressuring me into all that religious stuff again."

"Sammi, he only does that because he loves you. I do too, you know. By the way, I saw you rolling your eyes when Jimmy was sharing the Christmas story with the kids and telling them Jesus is the best gift they will ever receive. It's true. You have been running from it all your life, but you cannot outrun God, and you'll never be happy without Him."

"Don't start on me again, Candace. I'm not buying it. I know you and Dad think you know what's best for me, but you're wrong. You're both wrong. I've been living life and enjoying every minute of it. I don't have to answer to or worry about anyone else. I'm free, and I plan to stay that way."

"Sammi, I know you believe what you say, and don't get me wrong, but don't you ever wish you could find love? I mean real love."

"You know what I went through after Dusty and I broke up. You know how much I loved him, but he just didn't love me the same."

"Yes, I know how much you loved him, but you're wrong about him not loving you. He loved you more than any of those other guys ever could. That's why he insisted on waiting and why he wanted you to be a Christian. He knew you'd never be able to truly love him without Jesus in your own heart. Jesus is true love. The Bible says, 'No greater love hath any...'"

"Candace, I'm not in the mood for this. Can't we just sit here and talk about...I don't know...anything else? I don't want to ruin our time together arguing about religion. We hardly ever get to see each other."

"Okay, but only for now. I'm not going to give up on you."

Sammi let out a long, heavy sigh and rolled her eyes. "Yeah, I know."

The girls continued sharing stories about jobs, the children, old acquaintances and more. The night waned on, and soon it was three in the morning. Both girls yawned and then laughed at each other.

"I guess we better get some sleep," Candace said. "Jimmy and I will be heading back home tomorrow. The kids still get awful cranky trapped in the car for long periods of time, and without much sleep, I won't tolerate it as well. Good thing we planned some fun stops on the way. That should break up the monotony."

"I sure don't envy you traveling with two young children in a small car. It's a lot easier traveling alone."

"True, but the company is nice, at least, when they're not fighting." Candace laughed. "Well, good night, Sam."

"Goodnight, Can. See you in the morning."

The next morning, after a breakfast of super fluffy pancakes with peanut butter and syrup and a side of sausage links, Jimmy and Candace loaded their luggage and children into the car, said their goodbyes, and drove off down the road.

Sammi watched them leave and began to reflect on everything that had transpired. The thing that stuck foremost in her mind was the story of Jesus' birth. Of course she had heard it all before, but this time there was something different about it. Was it the way Jimmy read the account as if it were more than just a bedtime story? Was it because the children were so eager to hear the story and interested in it? Why was it so important to her best friend and her family? After all, it was just a children's story, wasn't it? Try as she might, Sammi couldn't get it out of her mind for nearly five days.

Chapter 6

By the time New Year's Eve rolled around, Sammi had been thinking that maybe she should give her father a call. Maybe she would even see about visiting him. Then, as she stopped by the dry cleaners for her party dress, she bumped into a stranger — walked straight into him without seeing him coming out the door — because her mind was still preoccupied with that silly Christmas story.

The stranger, lean and trim, dressed in a pin-striped suit and royal blue dress shirt with a silver neck-tie, simply smiled and cautioned, "You really have to watch out for people walking through these doors. Never know when you'll bump into the love of your life."

Sammi giggled, blushing, and then as she looked into his eyes, she saw her future self and knew he would be the one for her. "So sorry. I was just think-ing about..."

"Me. I hope." The stranger laughed at the per-plexed look on Sammi's face. "Oh. Forgive me. I've not even introduced myself. Name's Ron Hampton."

"Sammi Alexander. Pleased to meet you, Mr.

Hampton."

"Ron, please. Pleasure is all mine, Mrs. Alexander."

"Not Mrs. Just call me Sammi."

"Sammi?"

"Yes, Ron?"

"Are you free for dinner?"

"Well, as a matter of fact, I was just picking up my dress for a party tonight," Sammi responded. Then noticing the disappointed look on his face, she continued, "But if you are free, I would love for you to join me. My 'plus one' had to cancel last night, and I've no one to escort me."

"Oh that's too bad, for him. However, as it turns out, my plans changed last minute as well. Again the pleasure would be all mine to escort you. Just tell me when and where and I'm all yours, Lovely Sammi."

The two exchanged phone numbers and Sammi floated home without another thought of that silly Christmas story.

The night was perfect. Sammi looked smashing in her sequined, teal evening gown with sweetheart neckline. Her strawberry blonde hair was pulled up in a loose bun with curls hanging loosely, framing her face. Her blue eyes sparkled with a newfound excitement. She couldn't believe that she had met Ron on such a random chance encounter. If she had been just a minute earlier or later, they would never have run into each other.

Ron looked even more dashing in his tuxedo than he had in his pinstriped suit. When Sammi saw him getting out of his champagne colored Chevy Corvette, with his slightly wavy, salt and peppered black hair and clean shaven face, her heart seemed to skip a beat, and she had to remind herself to breathe.

Within the hour, they were dancing together at the New Year's Eve party in the vineyards of the best selling winery in Southern California.

"This is some party, Sammi! How did you become connected with such famous people like the Glendales?"

"It's all just part of the job." Then Sammi went on to explain how two years earlier, she had been the advertising executive for the Glendale Valley Wines campaign. Harvey Glendale had been so impressed with her advertising skills he had invited her to join them for all their holiday celebrations. Since she had no family in California, she accepted his invitation every time. They became closer than she ever had been with her own family. She had even begun to call Harvey "Pops," which always made him smile.

Sammi loved being an advertising executive and getting to meet people like Harvey and his wife Marlena. Sammi's mother passed away when Sammi was only a few months old, and for the past two years, Marlena became a mother figure to Sammi.

They talked on the phone almost daily and went to lunch together every Wednesday. Harvey and Marlena had only had two children of their own, twins. George had been killed in an automobile accident when he was twenty, and after that Julia found it too painful to come back home. Harvey and Marlena understood, but they missed their children deeply, and Sammi was a welcome relief.

Marlena approached the couple. "Who is this nice-looking, young fellow, Sammi? And where did you find him?"

"Ron, I'd like you to meet Marlena. Marlena, this is Ron Hampton. We just kind of bumped into each other. You know, one of those fateful kinds of meetings."

"Yes, the fate of Sammi not watching where she's going," laughed Ron. "It's very nice to meet you, Marlena."

"Nice to meet you too, Ron. Sammi does have a habit of forgetting to look out for others. Have you met my husband Harvey, yet? We both love Sammi as if she were our own daughter. We're the closest thing she has to family around here. There's Harvey over there by the wine tables. Come on, Ron. I'll introduce you to him."

Ron gave a quick glance at Sammi as Marlena grabbed his arm and began dragging him across the courtyard. Sammi smiled and shrugged, quickly mouthing, "Sorry," and followed after them.

Harvey was impressed with Ron's knowledge of wines and invited him to return to Glendale Valley with Sammi the following weekend for a more casual dinner, just the four of them.

Ron and Sammi seemed to be perfect for each other. Before the year was over, they were contemplating moving in together.

"You know I love you, Sammi, and we already spend most of our time together. It's silly of us to keep maintaining two apartments here when we could be sharing one. Will you just think it over? You don't have to answer yet. Before you decide, I want to give you this..." Ron handed her an envelope.

Sammi took the envelope from him with a perplexed look on her face. "This isn't the kind of gift I'd expect from someone asking me to move in. I mean, it can't be a ring or even a key."

"No, you're right. I know you're not ready for a ring and a key isn't in order yet, at least not until you decide. Just open it."

Cautiously, Sammi opened the envelope and pulled out two plane tickets. Looking at them, first she was shocked, and then a smile began to spread across her face. "Europe?"

"Yes, my love. I know how much you love Europe and have been wanting to go back. But this time you will be going with me. Doesn't that sound even better?" Ron teased, winking and rubbing his nose on hers.

"Oh, thank you! This is wonderful!" Sammi said, throwing her arms around his neck and kissing him.

"You are always so thoughtful! I love you, Ron."

Europe. That's where it all began to fall apart. Things were so great between the two of us, and then...Enter Dad. I got the call that Dad was having heart problems and wanted me to come home. We were having such a great time in Europe, no way did I want to end that to come back and be lectured about the whole God thing by Dad. Ron didn't understand. He thought I was heartless not to care more for the only "real" family I had left. Then the fights began, and the next thing I knew, we were agreeing to call it quits. After that, I definitely didn't want to see Dad, so it was back to Cali and working away my sorrows. How could I have been so wrong about Ron?

Chapter 7

"Hello, Cady?"

"Sammi? Hi!...Mom, Sammi is on the phone!...How's Europe? Did you buy me a special gift?"

"You know I always buy you something special, but I'm back in California now. I'll mail your gifts to you and your brother tomorrow. I miss you. How's school going?"

"School is great! Mrs. Cowan is the best teacher ever! I love her class. Canaan hates school though. He had to dissect a frog and said he almost barfed on the whole disgusting mess! Yuck!"

"Eww! I can imagine."

"Well, here's mom."

"Hello, Sammi? What's up? How's Europe?"

"Well, it was good, at first. I'm back in Cali now though."

"Already? What happened?"

"Dad," Sammi sighed. "Apparently he is having some health issues, and because I didn't drop everything and run to him, Ron thought I didn't care. He said if I couldn't care about my own father, how could I care about him? We started arguing about it more and more. Then he said we should probably reconsider our relationship."

"Oh, Sammi. I'm so sorry!"

"Well, I suppose since it didn't kill me, it must have made me stronger, right? Live and learn and get back to work. Someone has to pay the bills. Good thing I hadn't given up my apartment for him yet."

"If you had, and didn't have anywhere else to go, then maybe you could have come back here for a while."

"As much as I'd like to see you, Candace, I think I would have stayed here with Harvey and Marlena. You know, the job is here and all."

"You work way too much anyway. You need to have more fun. What did you say is wrong with your dad?"

"I think he said something like an enlarged heart. Have you ever heard of such a thing?"

"Hmmm...not really. How serious is it?"

"I'm not sure other than he said the doctor was making him give up his position as camp director. Too much stress and strain on his heart."

"Oh man! He loves that camp so much. That must be awful for him. Jimmy and I will have to go visit him and see what we can do to help."

"Thanks. I'm sure he will appreciate that."

"Anything we can do to help ol' Justin, but I'm sure it would be better if you were here."

"I just can't right now. Too much to do and I need to get over this Ron breakup. I'm already stressed to the max. I wouldn't be any help at all. Believe me."

"Okay, I'll keep you up-to-date on what's happening with the old man then."

"Thanks, Can. Talking to you always makes me feel better."

"Well, I love you, Sammi. Anything I can do to help you is my pleasure. I know you're stressed, but don't eat too much pasta. You know it's a pain to work off later."

Sammi looked down at the bowl of Alfredo she had just made and smiled. "You know me all too well. I promise not to eat too much of it, but it is the best comfort food."

"Just call me whenever you need."

"Will do. Love ya, Can."

"Love you too, Sam. Hang in there. I know Mr. Right is out there somewhere looking for you."

"I'm not so sure about that. I'll call you later this week and let you know how I'm doing."

"Sounds good to me. Later, then."

"Later."

Chapter 8

It was Sammi's thirty-fifth birthday. Candace had been hoping to surprise her in California, but the week before, Canaan had an accident playing touch football in the park after school. The trip to the emergency room proved that he didn't break any bones, but also took the extra funds that Candace had planned to use for the plane tickets.

"Happy birthday to you. Happy birthday..."

"Okay, alright! That's enough! I get it! You know you never were the best of singers, but I love you anyway, Candace." Sammi laughed. "I'm so glad you called. I just landed another big account and really wish you were here to help me celebrate."

"Funny you mention that. It was my plan to surprise you, but Canaan had other plans of going to the ER last week. He's fine, but finding that out cost me my plane ticket. So, SURPRISE! I didn't get to come out."

"Darn! That really stinks! I didn't even know you were planning to come."

"That's why they call it a surprise. Duh!"

"Oh, hahaha," Sammi laughed sarcastically. "Anyway, Marlena and Harvey are taking me out to dinner, and then a couple of women from work want to take me to a club. It should be a good birthday after all. If Dad would stop calling every hour, that is."

"He just misses you and wants you to know he loves you."

"I know, but I don't feel like talking to him today. He will only bring me down, pressuring me to come back there."

"Well, you definitely need to come visit us anyway."

"Too swamped at work right now, Can. Maybe someday soon."

"That's what you always say. I'll try not to hold my breath. I love you, Sammi, and I hope you have a great time tonight. Tell Marlena and Harvey I said hi."

"I'll tell them, and you can bet that I'll have fun. I'll call you tomorrow to share details. Love you, Can. Gotta go now. "

The next day, Sammi awoke to the bright sunlight flooding the room. Looking at the clock, she saw that it was already 12:38. Her mind was still reeling from all the activity. Dinner with the Glendales was delicious, and they gave her a beautiful tennis bracelet for her birthday. Then at the club, she was dancing with her friends when she accidentally bumped into someone. She turned around to apologize and froze. Her friends saw the look on her face and turned to look at the man Sammi was staring at. They had never seen him before, but they could tell she had.

"Well, now...Who is this?" questioned Carla, the gorgeous redhead with a dazzling smile.

"Dusty? Is it really you? When...How...What are you doing in this part of California?" Sammi stammered.

Carla looked questioningly at Stephani and Danielle as she mouthed, "Who's Dusty?" They both shrugged, shushed her, and motioned for her to pay attention.

"Sammi? Sammi Alexander? Wow! You look amazing," Dusty exclaimed. "Long time, no see. Right?"

"You've got that right, but you didn't answer my question. What brings you to Cali? I never thought I'd see you again. Especially in a club like this."

"I'm not exactly comfortable here, but I'm in the process of purchasing an accounting business in the area, and the owner insisted on showing me the town. She believes that the only way to be great in business is to know how to loosen up a bit from time to time. This is not my style of relaxation, though."

Interrupting, Danielle cleared her throat and stepped closer, tossing an arm around Sammi's shoulders, "Sammi, be a dear and introduce us. I don't know who this good-looking hunk is, but I could probably help him learn to loosen up."

"I seriously doubt that, Danielle. This is Dusty Newall. He's an old friend," Sammi stated.

"Well, any friend of Sammi's is a friend of..." Danielle began.

But Dusty cut her short, "Well, we were a bit more than friends, Sammi."

Danielle and the other girls looked even more confused and turned to Sammi for clarification.

"We dated for a while when we were teens," Sammi confessed. Dusty raised his eyebrow, crossed his arms, and waited for Sammi to continue. "Alright! Dusty and I were engaged after high school."

At this point, Stephani made the connection and stepped in front of Danielle. "I think it's time to let these two catch up on old times. Besides, I think that cute guy over there is checking you out, Danielle. Come on. Catch you later, Sammi."

"Really, you don't have to leave..." Sammi started, but Stephani had already locked arms with Danielle and Carla, and the three were walking across the room. Sammi turned to Dusty. "I guess it's you and me then. Do you want to go get some coffee and talk?"

"You want to leave? Isn't this supposed to be like your birthday party or something?"

"You remember that it's my birthday?"

"Of course I do. Every year."

"Wow, really? That's amazing. Thank you. But this party is not as happening as I hoped it would be. So, yes, let's go get some coffee."

They left the club and headed down the street to

a corner cafe where they chatted about life until the waitress told them it was closing time.

"You mean, it's already two a.m.? Wow, time flies, right?" Dusty said. "I'll have some explaining to do tomorrow for running out on Micah like that, but she'll be glad it was for an old friend. At least, she'll know I have friends now," he laughed.

"I'm just glad that I have the day off and get to sleep late. That is if Candace doesn't call me too early for the birthday party scoop."

"Candace? You two are still best of friends then?"

"You know it! Wouldn't want my life without her, even with the miles between us. She'll be glad to hear that I ran into you, I'm sure."

"Well, tell her I said hi."

"I will. Thanks for the coffee, Dusty. It was great seeing you, but I better get home."

"Great seeing you too. Let me walk you to your car." The two continued to talk as they strolled back down the block. At Sammi's car, Dusty reached into his breast pocket and pulled out a card. "Here's my card, in case you want to get together again sometime. Just give me a call. Goodnight, Sammi. Or should I say, 'Good morning'?" he laughed.

"I think 'goodnight' will do. Bye, Dusty."

The cell phone ringing on the nightstand tore her from her reminiscing.

"Hey, Candace."

"Good afternoon, Sunshine! How did your birthday go?"

"You're never going to believe how it ended," Sammi smiled as she told her best friend all about her night out and how she bumped into Dusty, "of all people," at the club.

"You have to call him! It's like fate that the two of you met again after all these years and you're both still single. You know God works in mysterious ways. This could be your second chance for happiness with Dusty. Tell me you're planning to see him again!"

"Maybe...Wow! I still can't believe it was him. He's still as nice as ever. And as nice-looking too. He still remembers my birthday! Can you believe that?"

"Of course, I can. You still don't realize how much he loved you back then, do you? He probably never stopped loving you. When you call him, make sure you say hi from me," Candace teased, knowing her best friend would be calling to see Dusty again. "I really wish I could have been there, but now I see why I couldn't. You two wouldn't have had the opportunity to reconnect if I was with you."

"True. I couldn't have left my bestie if she came all the way out to Cali for me."

"Well, I hate to cut this call so short, but I have to take Canaan to the doctor for another checkup. He's still having a lot of pain. I hope they didn't miss a hairline fracture or something."

"Gosh, I hope not! Tell both the kids and Jimmy hi and thanks for the birthday wishes. I better get myself out of bed and find some coffee. Later, Can."

"Later, Sam." Both ladies chuckled as they hung up.

Chapter 9

By the time Wednesday rolled around, Sammi had been so deep into her latest project, that she hadn't thought of much else. The television news was playing in the background as she worked late in her apartment. She was so engrossed in drawing her rough sketch that she nearly missed the story, but when the anchor mentioned Dusty's name, Sammi's attention was caught. She looked at the TV just in time to see Dusty shaking hands with a young, brunette lady during a press conference.

She must be the accountant who brought him to the club the other day, she thought. The story was about Dusty becoming the new owner of the accounting firm. Sammi picked up her phone and dialed his number.

"Dusty Newall, CPA. How can I help you?"

"Hi! It's Sammi. I just saw you on the news and wanted to call and congratulate you on the new business purchase. I'm happy for you."

"Thanks, Sammi. It was touch and go for a bit, but, whew, what a relief that it's a done deal now."

"Maybe we could get together to celebrate later

this week."

"I would like that, but it will have to be Friday. I'm heading out of town Saturday. My aunt and uncle are celebrating their 40th anniversary, and Mom wants me to be there."

"Wow! Forty years! I can't even imagine. That's longer than I've been alive."

"Yes, I know. Me too. Are you free Friday then?"

"I'm having dinner with a client, so it will have to be around 8:00. Will that be too late for you since you're leaving the next day?"

"I think I can manage. After all, I'm pretty good at sleeping on planes."

"If there aren't any screaming babies on board, right?"

"Don't say that! You'll jinx me!" Dusty laughed.

"Sorry. So I'll see you Friday at eight?"

Dusty agreed to pick her up, and Sammi gave him her address. As she hung up the phone, she marveled at the events that had transpired over the recent weeks. *I can't believe my luck of running into Dusty again after all these years, she thought. What if Candace is right and it's more than just luck?..Nah!*

Finishing dinner with her client, Sammi was elated. Her proposal was warmly accepted and it truly looked like the owners of the newest theme park were going to hire her. Rushing back to her apartment, she thought, *It's possible that Dusty and I may be having a double celebration tonight, but I better wait until we sign the contract on this ad.*

A quick change of clothes, a tossing of her hair, and a fresh touch-up of make-up, and she was ready when the doorbell rang. She opened the door with a smile.

"Wow!" Dusty exclaimed. "how is it possible that you look more astonishing every day?"

"Oh, please," Sammi said sarcastically, rolling her eyes. "You are such a kiss up. But thank you."

"I hope you didn't eat so much that you don't have room for dessert and coffee. I want to take you to my favorite little cafe."

"Actually, I barely got to eat anything while pitching my idea, so dessert sounds fantastic."

"I'm sorry you didn't get to eat, but I'm glad too. How did it go?"

"Extremely well. I'm pretty sure they want to hire me."

"Hopefully we'll be having another celebration when I get back then," Dusty smiled and winked at her as he helped her with her coat and led the way out to his midnight blue Toyota Tacoma. Twenty-three minutes later, they were sitting in a fifties-style burger diner sharing a huge brownie fudge sundae covered by a mountain of whipped cream topped with chopped nuts.

"Mmmmm! This was worth missing out on most of my dinner," Sammi declared.

"I remembered how much you love brownie fudge sundaes, and this place has the best I've ever tasted."

"How do you remember so much about me?"

"You have always been a very special person in my life, since that first summer I came to Camp Green Forest. I truly loved you, you know. One of my biggest regrets in life is that we called it quits instead of getting married. I hope it's not too soon in our reunion for me to confess such a thing."

"It's soon, alright, but not too soon. I sort of feel the same way. I guess I didn't realize it until I saw you again on my birthday. I must have been repressing it, refusing to think about it, and just trying to move on. Seeing you has made me realize I never got over you."

"Sammi, I'm so happy to hear you say that. I hope we can continue to rekindle our relationship when I get back."

"I don't see why we can't."

"Wonderful!" The two finished the sundae and continued talking for nearly two and a half hours, sipping coffee, and sharing stories of their lives for the past sixteen years.

Dusty drove her back to her apartment and walked her to her door. As he leaned in to kiss her goodnight, Sammi asked if he'd like to come in for a drink.

"Yes, but no," Dusty replied. "I still believe in doing things the right way. I wouldn't want to ruin this second chance with you. I hope you understand."

"Not exactly, but I do respect your desire. Thanks for the sundae and your company. I hope you have a safe trip and enjoy your family's celebration. Call me when you get back?"

"Most definitely. Goodnight, Sammi Lou."

"Goodnight, Dusty Dude."

The two laughed at the use of their old nicknames as they hugged and Dusty walked away. Inside her apartment, Sammi sighed, smiling and leaning against the closed door. She silently hoped that this time things would work out between them.

Chapter 10

"Oh! How wonderful! Sammi, I'm so excited for you!" Candace squealed into the phone the next day as Sammi told her about dessert with Dusty and their confessions of affection. "I know fate brought you two back together!"

"Mom, what's the matter?" Cady asked in the background.

"Nothing, honey. Nothing is wrong at all! Sammi is dating Dusty again. It's just so exciting!"

"Dusty? Who's Dusty?"

"I'll tell you about him later. Right now, I'm on the phone."

Sammi laughed, "Yes, you are. I think you are more excited than I am about this renewal. I won't have a lot of free time over the next few weeks though if the amusement park people hire me to do their ads."

"Of course they are going to hire you! You are awesome at creating ads! But you better make time to talk to Dusty. Don't let him get away again!"

"Yes, I think you're right about that." Sammi continued to give Candace details about her clients and

Dusty.

Harvey and Marlena's thirty-fifth wedding anniversary was the following week. Naturally they wanted Sammi to come to their celebration, and naturally Sammi wanted Dusty to be her date for the occasion.

"So, you're taking me to meet 'the parents'?" he teased, using his fingers to put air quotes around "the parents" as he said it.

"Yes, I think it's about time you met them, don't you?"

"What if they don't approve of me? After all, I'm one of those goody-goody boys and they're wine people."

"They will love you. Everybody does. Besides, you make me happy and that's what's important to them."

Of course, Sammi was right. Dusty was a big hit with Harvey and Marlena. They even hinted that maybe someday it would be Dusty and Sammi celebrating thirty-five years of marriage.

"Oh, now, don't rush things. We just got back together," Sammi cautioned.

"That doesn't matter. When it's right, it's right. Marlena and I had only known each other for two months before we got married. And here we are celebrating a milestone most couples never see these days."

"He's right, dear. If you know Dusty is the one, there's no reason to wait," Marlena added.

"Hey, I'm standing right here," Dusty teased. "Don't I have any say in this?"

"Why? Are you objecting?" Sammi asked.

"No, not at all, but you know I like to consult a Higher Authority before making big decisions."

"I like that in a man. I'm glad to hear that about you, Dusty," Harvey interjected. "Now, you definitely have my permission. As long as you get the Big Guy's permission, that is."

"Wait a minute. You're agreeing with Dusty on religion? How did I never know you were religious people?" Sammi wondered.

"Well, sweetheart," Marlena began, "we knew your feelings about God, and we understand that talking about Him sometimes pushes people away from Him. We never wanted to do that, so we just kept it quiet. Gaining a person's trust is often more important in leading them to Christ than preaching the Bible is."

"Wow! Well said," Dusty added.

"But you're wine people. How does that work?" questioned Sammi.

"Jesus made wine too. Don't you know? Some say it's good for you. I believe it's like anything else; it depends if you abuse it or not," Harvey explained.

"Hmm. I'll have to give that some thought I guess," Sammi contemplated.

Marlena locked her arm with Sammi's and spoke, "In the meantime, there's a party going on here. Let's celebrate the love I have for this old guy here." She motioned with her thumb toward Harvey and drew Sammi and the guys back toward the other guests.

As the evening progressed, Dusty began thinking more and more about the possibility of marrying Sammi someday. *If only she were a Christian, there would be no hesitation on my part. I wonder if she has given that any thought lately.*

The next several weeks were a whirlwind. Sammi was hired for the ad, and between that and the other campaigns she was working on and making time to see Dusty at least twice a week, she wasn't sure where she was heading half the time.

"Maybe this isn't the best time for me to bring this up..." Dusty began.

"What? Do you have to leave town or something?" Sammi was curious what could be making Dusty so serious.

"Well, my mother received a call the other day. It seems your dad is really not doing well. He's reaching out to the former camp workers, looking for someone to come and help him get the place back in order. Mom thought I might want to come back for a week and help out. Please, don't roll your eyes like that, Sammi. I feel like this is something I should do. Your dad was always good to us, and I never had a chance to repay him. You know, if he hadn't hired my mom to cook that first summer, well...we were flat broke and headed downhill fast. Mom never wanted me to know how hard it was without my dad around, but I knew."

"I understand your desire to do something for all he did for you and your mom. I guess, if you can get away from the accounting firm for a week, I can't stop you. I'm not saying I like the idea. A whole week, huh? What will I do without you?"

Dusty laughed. "Gee, I wonder. Oh, yeah! You'll probably work straight through without even noticing that I'm not here."

"Oh, I'll notice! I'll probably have brownie fudge sundae withdrawals since you won't be able to bring me one and force me to stop working long enough to help you eat it." Sammi giggled.

"Hey! A guy's gotta do what a guy's gotta do."

"Just do me one favor."

"Anything for you, Sammi Lou."

"Don't tell my father that we are dating. It's probably best that you don't even mention me. All right?"

"All right, but one day I hope to take you back there with me. Mom misses you too."

"We'll see. Maybe someday, but don't hold your breath. So when are you leaving?"

"Sunday evening. We can go out Saturday night before I leave, and I'll be back the next Saturday afternoon. You'll barely have time to miss me, or my brownie fudge sundaes." Dusty smirked and pulled Sammi closer to him for a kiss. "My Sammi Lou, do you know how I feel about you?"

"Yes, I think so. Is it something like the way toast

loves butter?"

"Toast and butter? Where did you come up with that one?"

"I'm not sure. It just popped into my head for some reason."

"Well, I kind of like it," he said as he pulled her in for another kiss, "but do you know what I think works better?"

"What's that, Dusty Dude?"

"I love you better than brownie loves fudge."

"Aww! You are the best, aren't you?" Sammi kissed him again.

"The best? I don't know about that, but I've got to be pretty close. I hate to say it, but it is getting late. I've got a big day tomorrow to wrap things up before I leave. Pick you up Saturday at five?"

"That will be perfect. See you then. Goodnight, Dusty."

"Goodnight, Sammi." He kissed her once more before allowing her to close the door.

When Sammi opened the door Saturday evening, she knew right away that something wasn't right. Dusty could never hide his true feelings from her.

"What is it? I know something is bothering you?"

"My mother called this morning. Your father has had an episode of some kind. He's been in the hospital, but should get released in the morning. In light of this latest news, though, he won't be working on the camp next week, so I don't need to go back. I'm all yours, it seems."

"Dad's going to be alright, isn't he?"

"For now, at least, he should be."

"Then that's good. And I don't have to miss you next week? That's even better."

"I agree with you there. I wasn't looking forward to being so far away from you, but we really should think about making a trip out there to see the old man."

"You're probably right, but you know how swamped I am with my clients right now. Mr. Rogers wants me to take on another big project next week, too. Some mega store is looking to expand their market."

"Wow! You are the super woman of the ad world! I don't blame Mr. Rogers for wanting you to be in charge of all the big accounts, but, Sammi, sometimes you have to say no to other people so you can take care of yourself, and your loved ones."

"Even though Dad and I didn't see eye-to-eye on things, I do love him, and I guess I should try to get out there. Maybe I'll start with a phone call. I can probably squeeze in a call next week."

"Well, that's a start, I guess. Any time you're ready for the trip, let me know. I'd love to take you by Mom's place for a visit, too."

"Your mom always did love me, didn't she?"

"Yes, but not as much as brownie loves fudge," Dusty teased as he grasped her hand and brought it gently to his lips for a light kiss.

"Oh, yeah? You want to bet?" Sammi teased back

before giving him a big hug and rubbing her nose against his.

"But seriously, I'd love to make the trip back with you. How about as soon as this big mega store ad is pitched?"

"All right. We will shoot for then. I guess I better get to work on that or we will never get to take that trip. Will we?"

"Hey, I can take a hint. I'll get out of your hair and let you work your magic. Goodnight, Brownie Lou."

"Night, Dusty Fudge."

Chapter 11

Sammi got the phone call from Candace the day before her big mega store ad proposal.

"Hey, Candace. What's up? Is everything alright?"

"Well, sadly, no, Sammi. I don't know how to say this, so I'm just going to be blunt. I'm afraid that your father's heart finally gave out, and he's gone."

"What?! Oh, no! I had planned to come, but work is always so demanding. I've got a huge presentation tomorrow. Do you know when the funeral will be? Who is making the arrangements?"

"Henry Barnes is handling all of that and should be calling you soon. I love you, Sammi, and I'm praying for you. We all are. You can stay in our guest room while you're here. Let me know if you need anything else."

"Thanks, Candace. You are the best friend I could ever have. I'll call you later and let you know when I'll be there."

"Okay. Take care, Sammi."

Sammi could feel the tears welling up in her eyes as she hung up the phone. *Oh, Dad. Why did I have to be so busy and so stubborn?*

Henry Barnes had been the family attorney for the past twenty-five years. He had practically watched Sammi grow up and was a close friend of the family.

"You will need to come home for the funeral and the reading of the will. Again, I'm so sorry, Sammi. I know he had hoped to see you before the end, but..."

"When do I need to be there?"

"I've set the funeral up for Saturday. I thought it would be a little easier for you to make it in time that way. You'll need to stay a few days though, so you can attend the reading and go through some of his belongings and decide what you want to do with everything. I'll be here to help you anyway I can."

"Thank you, Henry. I appreciate that. I'll book a flight for Friday afternoon and give you a call when it lands."

"That will be fine, Sammi. I'll meet you at the airport if you need a ride."

"Thank you, but it will probably be better if I just rent a car for the length of my stay. I'll let my boss know I'll need at least a week off."

"Why don't you let me bring your father's truck for you to use instead. After all, technically it's yours now. No sense renting what you already have available. Also, it may take a little longer than a week, so keep your leave of absence open. I'll see you Friday."

"Good idea on both counts. Thanks again, Henry. See you Friday."

Sammi hung up and then called Bob Rogers, her boss at the advertising agency.

"I'm so sorry to hear that, Sammi. Take as long as you need. Just stay in touch. I'm assuming you will be able to work some from there if needed."

"Yes, definitely. I won't be leaving until Friday, so tomorrow's mega store proposal is still on. While I'm gone, I'll check in with you each day and email my progress on the other accounts. I'll be back as soon as possible."

"No need to rush things. I'm sure there are decisions that will require some consideration time. With today's technology, you can do most of your job from there. I only ask that you get back in time for your next presentation."

"That won't be a problem. I don't want to stay in that place any longer than necessary."

"I know how you feel about your hometown, but this is your father's funeral and I'm afraid there will be more to deal with than you realize. Let me know if you need any advice. I've been through this with my own parents, so I can help."

"Thanks, Bob, but Henry, Dad's lawyer, will be helping me with everything. He's an old family friend and all."

"I'm glad to hear that. Have a safe trip then."

"Safe and quick, I hope. See you soon, Bob."

Sammi couldn't wait for Dusty to call that evening. She needed to talk to him. She knew he would want to know and that he would try to go with her.

"Oh, Sammi. I'm so sorry. I'll be over as soon as I can. I just need to wrap up a few last minute things here. I'll pick up some pasta from Guido's on the way."

Forty minutes later, they were sitting at Sammi's kitchen table eating chicken Parmesan and garlic bread.

"Thank you so much for the food. Guido always has the best pasta. This really hits the spot."

"Anything for my sweet brownie. Now tell me what happened."

Sammi explained what the family attorney had told her. He agreed that she needed to go, and he really wished he could go with her, but he didn't think he could get free from work for a couple of days. He would try his best and at the very least fly out for the funeral.

The mega store proposal was a huge success, and before Sammi knew it, it was already Friday. Time to fly back to Camp Green Forest. As she boarded the plane and prepared for the flight, she sighed. *Well, at least I will get to spend some time with Candace and the kids. I can at least look forward to that part of the trip.*

Two hours later, the plane was landing. Sammi took a deep breath, stepped off the plane, and headed out front where Henry was waiting with the truck. Within fifteen minutes, she had dropped Henry back at his office and was knocking on the door of Candace's log cabin.

Cady opened the door. "SAMMI!" she exclaimed, excited to see Sammi again after so long. "Sammi! Yea! You made it! Mom! Sammi's here!" She screamed as she grabbed Sammi in a huge hug. "It's so good to see you! Oh! I'm sorry about your dad."

"Cady, you're growing up too fast! How old are you now? Twenty?"

"Haha. No, you know better than that. How long do you get to stay with us?"

"That all depends on how long it takes to get things all squared away. Probably at least a week."

"Well, I am sorry about your dad, but I'm really glad you're here," Cady said as she gave Sammi another hug.

"Me too, kiddo. Me too," Sammi sighed.

Candace walked in and gave Sammi a hug. "There's my best friend! I've missed you so much, Sammi. You've got to visit more often and for better reasons."

"I know, Can. I'm just always so busy. It's so good to see you guys though. Even under these circumstances."

"I wish you could have come sooner. Your dad kept asking for you, over and over."

"There was just no way I could break free with that big megastore proposal looming over my head. I still have to keep the bills paid. I hope he wasn't too upset with me."

"I don't want to make you feel bad, but yes, he was heartbroken. His only hope was that maybe he will see you in heaven someday."

"At this point, I wouldn't hold my breath. You know that's not anything I have time to worry about."

"Sammi, I know, but I pray you will before it's too late. Anyway, do you want to bring your stuff into the guest room? I got it all ready for you."

"Thanks. I appreciate you letting me stay here. I just don't want to be alone out there on the camp-grounds."

"I understand. It's no problem at all. The kids were so excited to hear that you'd be staying here for a few days."

Just then Canaan came walking in. Sammi could see that he was trying to control his excitement and act like a too cool teenage boy. "Hey, Sammi. Good to see you," he said with a slight wave of his right hand.

"Hey? Are you kidding me? You get over here and give me a hug! You're not too big yet for me to tackle."

Laughing, Canaan scoffed, "Ya, right! You can't take me down."

"You want to find out? Get over here, you little turkey."

"Alright, alright. But only because you have enough to deal with now; you don't need to add getting whipped by a teenager to your list of worries," Canaan teased as he walked over and hugged Sammi. She scrubbed his noggin before letting him out of a headlock. "Hey, now! That's enough, Sammi. Let me go!"

"Uh huh! I thought you were all big and bad." Sammi kidded.

"Just don't let my friends know. I've got a rep to maintain, you know," Canaan whispered, smoothing his hair back in place.

They all laughed. Then Candace interjected, "Alright, kiddos. Let's let Sammi put her things away and freshen up for dinner. I've ordered pizza for tonight."

"Yes, pizza!" Both kids exclaimed in unison.

Chapter 12

As Sammi sat waiting to have her truck, formerly her dad's truck, serviced at the local Chevy dealership, she started to realize just how serious her dad's condition must have been. *I can't believe that the camp is in such bad shape. Dad never let things go like this before. And the way that he cherished this old truck and babied it all the time, for him to not get it serviced on time...Man, he must have really been having a tough time getting around. I wish I wouldn't have been so stubborn. I should have come back to visit before...*

Just then, an older lady approached her. "Sammi, is that you?"

"Yes. I'm sorry. Do I know y..." Then with sudden realization, Sammi smiled. "Mrs. Bakstrum? Oh my goodness! I haven't seen you in years. How are you?"

"I'm fine, dear. It's so good to see you. I heard you were back in town."

"Only for a week, or maybe two. I didn't even know you were still around. I'm glad to see that you are, of course, but last I heard, you weren't doing very well and were placed in the nursing home."

"Oh, that was a terrible time! I had cancer, you

know. The doctor said I needed constant care after the chemo had left me so weak. But I refused to give up. 'Lord,' I prayed, 'I know you still have plans to use this old broken down body in some mighty way, but You have to help me heal and get out of this nursing home first.' I just kept praying that, believing it, and working with the physical therapist until I was well enough to go home."

"You're still the same strong-faithed, sweet-hearted lady I remember that used to teach the girls' Sunday school class. I will never forget how you were always so loving to each of us."

"That's right, dear. I knew you were only there because your dad forced you to attend every week, but I also knew the Lord loved you as much as He loved me, and it was my duty -- no, my privilege -- to share that love with you. Tell me, are you going to church anywhere these days?"

Somewhat ashamed, Sammi replied, "No, I haven't gone to church for many years. Dusty has been asking me to go with him, but God and I never really agreed on much. I guess I blame God for not having my mom around all those years. I don't understand why He would take a mother away from a tiny baby who needed her so much."

"Oh, honey, I don't understand that either, but I do know that it's not God's fault. The devil likes to attack God's children and drive a wedge between them and God's will. That way they aren't working for the kingdom. Remember how I taught you about putting on the full armor of God so you could stand against the attacks of the devil. There's a spiritual battle taking place and we are caught in the middle of it."

"Yes, I remember you said that almost every Sunday. I just never really understood. I still don't, really."

"Why don't you come over to my house for lunch tomorrow so we can talk about this some more?"

"That would be nice, but I am already having lunch with Candace tomorrow."

"Bring her along too. I would love to see her again too. You girls always were inseparable."

"Alright, I will ask her. I bet she will be glad to come. She used to say you were the sweetest, most caring lady in the church."

Mrs. Bakstrum quickly jotted something on a slip of paper and handed it to Sammi. "Here's my address, and my phone number in case you need to cancel, otherwise I will expect to see both of you girls at, let's say, 12:30 tomorrow."

"Thank you, Mrs. Bakstrum. That's perfect. See you then."

A young lady approached. "Ms. Alexander? Your truck is ready."

Rising to her feet, Sammi hugged Mrs. Bakstrum. "I'll call if we are not able to make it tomorrow. Bye, Mrs. Bakstrum."

Mrs. Bakstrum replied, "See you tomorrow, dear," as Sammi followed the young lady back to the service desk. Mrs. Bakstrum quickly prayed, *Lord, soften Sammi's heart and help her be receptive to You and Your word.*

The next day, the two friends arrived at Mrs. Bakstrum's house just before 12:30. Mrs. Bakstrum looked so quaint with her upswept hair and periwinkle blue dress. Her radiant smile made her look much younger than she was as she assured the girls that they were a delightful sight for this lonely widow.

"I don't get a lot of visitors these days. I am so glad that you girls stopped by," Mrs. Bakstrum declared as she placed a plate of finger sandwiches on the table in front of the girls. "I hope sandwiches are all right with the two of you. These are water chestnut and tomato with swiss; I'm slightly famous around here for these, you know."

The two girls snickered as they both grabbed a sandwich. "Yes, we have heard that. These were always my favorite at church potluck dinners," Candace said.

"Mine too," Sammi added. "Now I'm really glad I bumped into you at the car dealer's yesterday."

"I knew it was you right away, Sammi," Mrs. Bakstrum said. "You look just like your mother did. She was such a lovely young lady. I'm sure you miss her as much as the rest of us."

"Yes," Sammi replied sadly. "There have been so many times in my life that I wished she had been there to help raise me. Dad did the best he could, I guess, but I'm sure my life would have been different with a mother's touch."

Trying to lighten the mood, Candace interjected, "But hey, you always had my mom and me to help. That should count for something."

"True. You guys were great. I definitely wouldn't have made it through high school without my bestie and her mom," Sammi said giving Candace a hug. "Don't forget my grandmother was there as much as she could have been, too," turning back to Mrs. Bakstrum, she continued, "but I have often had many questions about the type of woman my mother was. Dad and Grandma always found it too difficult to talk about her. Maybe you could tell me a little more about her."

"I'd be happy to, dear. The thing I remember most is her love for that camp. From the first year she went as the pianist, she had a special place in her heart for it and the impact it made on the lives of so many children. I think that is the main reason she was attracted to your father."

Sammi seemed a little shocked. "Really? I never knew that. I thought Dad only cared so much for the camp because it was his family's way of life. Now I see that he had another reason -- because it had meant so much to my mom and he loved her so deeply."

"Everyone knew that he loved your mother more than his own life. He was devastated when she passed. You were so tiny, not quite six months old, and you needed him almost as much as he needed you. You were his reason to carry on. You know, honey, it really hurt him that you didn't come back home when he was so sick." Mrs. Bakstrum could see that Sammi was troubled by the turn this conversation was taking, but she knew that Sammi needed to hear the truth. "Sammi, I didn't invite you over to lecture you on the importance of family, but you have to believe your father wanted only the best for you. You were all that he had left in this world, and he wanted to make sure you would be joining him in the next one too."

"Thank you for sharing this with me, Mrs. Bakstrum. I do appreciate it, and you've given me something to think about," Sammi said thoughtfully.

"And thank you for these wonderful sandwiches," Candace chimed in.

"Well, just wait until you see what I've prepared for dessert," Mrs. Bakstrum replied with a sheepish grin. "Let me get it."

The girls stayed and chatted with Mrs. Bakstrum for another hour, enjoying cheesecake and cappuccino. It was the most relaxing time Sammi had enjoyed in years. She just felt a sense of peace in Mrs. Bakstrum's house that she hadn't felt since she was a young child. She actually felt a growing sadness as she hugged Mrs. Bakstrum goodbye and promised to stay in touch.

As they drove down the recently paved road to Candace's log cabin house, Candace spoke up, "I know it's not your favorite topic, but Mrs. Bakstrum was right about your father wanting you to join him in heaven some day."

"Candace, not now, please. I already have so much to think about in my life. When I get back to California, I have to meet with, not one, but two new clients and develop proposals for their products. Then there's Dusty. He is still hinting that we should tie the knot, but I'm just not ready to complicate my life that much more."

"Well, Sammi, you guys have been dating for over a year now, plus way back when too. You're not getting any younger. We're already thirty-six! You are going to have to settle down sometime."

"I don't want to 'settle' for less than everything I want though."

"You shouldn't, and I'm still praying you will find God's best for your life."

"There you go again!"

"Okay, let's change the subject. Have you thought about what you are going to do with the camp now that you are the owner?"

"Ugh! Honestly, no. Right now it just seems like another complication in my life."

"Whatever you decide, I'll support you. Something to think about though is that Jimmy and I are willing to be caretakers and lead counselors for you if you should decide to reopen it. We will even help you clean the place up and get it back in shape."

"Thanks, Can. I appreciate that. I know the camp means a lot to the both of you. I'll keep that offer in mind when I make my decision. Who knows? It may even be time to sell the 'family business' to a new family."

"If that's the case, let us make the first bid. That camp is a huge part of our lives. Jimmy and I wouldn't even know each other if it hadn't been for that summer when we were seventeen."

"I know it, and I will definitely give you the first chance to buy it if that's what I decide to do."

As they pulled into the driveway, Cady ran out of the house, yelling, "Mom! Where have you been? I'm starving! What's for supper?"

Canaan wasn't far behind her, asking, "Did you bring us a pizza?"

With a huge sigh, Candace teased Sammi, "Who are these kids? Are they yours?"

"Ha, ha, ha. I should be so lucky," Sammi replied with a hint of sarcasm. "Come on. We better feed these poor neglected children. I bet they haven't eaten in seven days."

"In the house, kiddos. It's time mama taught you how to fend for yourselves."

Chapter 13

By the middle of the next week, Sammi was extremely stressed. The funeral had been a simple graveside service with only a few close friends in attendance. Dusty had come back home to be there for Sammi, but he was staying at his mother's place in town to give her some space to deal with everything.

As much as Sammi loved Candace and the gang, she knew she needed to spend some time alone at the camp to sort through her father's belongings and to decide what she would do with the family campground now that it was all hers. "Candace, I really enjoy staying here with you and your family, but if I don't spend some time cleaning dad's house, I'll never get back to Cali. Even as understanding as Bob is, eventually he will have to fire me when I don't return."

"No doubt about that. You know I'd be happy to come out there and help you sort through it all."

"Thank you so much, but it's probably best for me to do this alone."

"Well, if you change your mind, I'm only a holler

away. I can bring Canaan and Cady to help with the heavy lifting and carrying, too. You don't have to go through this alone."

"Okay, if I need help, I will call you," Sammi agreed, winking.

Justin didn't have that many personal belongings. He put most of his money into improving and expanding the camp each year. His clothes, Sammi decided, should be donated to Goodwill along with his dishes and such. Sammi spent half a day cleaning the refrigerator, cabinets, and closets and loading the truck with the donation items. Then she took a walk around the grounds, making a list of work that needed to be done.

I can't run this place alone. There's just no way. I don't even have the desire to stay here. This isn't what I want for my life. The ad agency is my life, and I love my beach house in California. Maybe I should put the campground on the market and let someone else worry about fixing all this mess. I wonder how serious Candace was about that. Well, I know she's serious, but I wonder if she and Jimmy can afford it. Maybe I'll have to make them a deal. I sure can't run this place from California.

When Dusty arrived the following evening, Sammi discussed the idea with him first.

"I can't think of anyone who would be better for taking over this camp. Jimmy and Candace both love the place, almost as much as your dad did. But are you really sure you want to let it go? I know it's not your ideal lifestyle, but it is your family legacy."

"Candace is practically family, and I know it would mean so much to them. They will do right by my 'family legacy' as you say. There's definitely no way I can do what needs to be done when I'm in California."

"You know, if we were married, you and I could move back here, and the four of us could work together to whip this place into shape in no time and then manage it together. Who needs California when you have Camp Green Forest?"

"Whoa! Slow down there. Too much too fast. I need Cali. It's my sanity right now. The only reason I am able to get through this is because I know soon I'll be back to work on the ads and I won't have time to think about Dad being gone. I didn't even call him before he..." Sammi wiped a tear from her eye as Dusty pulled her into his arms.

"Okay, I'll give you some time on the marrying me part, and we don't have to give up Cali. Just please don't feel like you have to be so strong. It's alright to cry. It's normal. I know it was hard for you to agree with your dad and that kept you from being close to him for way too long. He loved you so much that I'm sure he forgave you. You have to forgive yourself, too."

"I know you're right. I'm just ashamed of myself. It seems so childish now to let one silly little thing come between my dad and me. Aren't grown ups supposed to agree to disagree and get along?"

"Well, yes, but we are prideful humans and think our way is the only way. It tore us apart before, and even though I won't change my standards and beliefs, I'm also not going to let you get away again. Why don't we meet for lunch with Jimmy and Candace tomorrow and see what they say about taking over ownership of the camp? My flight doesn't leave until 3. Then I'll come back as soon as I can to help you tie up all the loose ends here."

"That sounds like a wonderful plan, except for the part about you leaving without me. I had hoped to be done here by now. Mr. Barnes was right about it taking longer than I thought. Bob is already calling me every other day, questioning me about how things are going. I know he's really wondering how soon I can be back in the office."

"You've been working too hard here and trying to keep everything afloat in the ad business. You have to remember to stop and breathe at least once a day, too. Why don't we make some pasta and watch a movie tonight?"

"Pasta! Yes! But I'm filthy from roaming through the woods earlier. Maybe you could do the cooking while I take a quick shower? You know you're the better cook anyway."

"I don't have a problem with that. Go get yourself cleaned up for supper, young lady!"

Dressed in comfy sweats and a long-sleeve t-shirt, Sammi entered the dining room fifteen minutes later to find the table set, complete with lit candles.

Dusty walked in carrying two plates of tortellini Alfredo with breadsticks.

"Mmmm! That smells so wonderful! You're amazing! I would still be in there trying to find a pan to cook it in." Sammi laughed.

"Grazie, signora. Now please to have a seat," Dusty teased in his best Italian accent.

"This is exactly what I needed tonight. Thank you so much for taking care of me, Dusty Dude."

"My pleasure, sweet Sammi Lou."

The two enjoyed their pasta, laughing and talking. They opted to skip watching a movie since it was so late and Dusty had to drive back to his mother's house.

"Drive safe. I'll see you for lunch tomorrow then?"

"Definitely. Good night, Sammi."

"Night, Dusty."

The four friends met for lunch at their old hangout, Dominique's Pizza Palace, and discussed the options for the camp. Jimmy and Candace were elated that Sammi wanted them not only to be directors of the camp but also owners. They agreed on a plan and a price for transferring a part-ownership that fit into Jimmy and Candace's budget. They would be in full charge of the camp while Dusty and Sammi were in California, but Sammi would provide funding for the needed improvements and be in charge of the advertising to encourage more teens to attend the camp. Dusty volunteered to come out before the next summer to help lend a hand fixing up the place. It was a perfect setup.

By the time the details were all settled, it was time for Dusty to catch his plane back to California, but he promised Sammi it shouldn't take more than a few days, a week tops, to take care of the necessary business items at the firm. He'd be back as soon as possible. As he left for the airport, Candace put her arm around her best friend.

"Hey, cheer up, Sammi. You still have me and Jimmy here to help you out until Dusty gets back. What can we do for you?"

"Thanks, Candace. Do you think we could get the kids to help us load up the rest of the stuff that I've decided to donate to Goodwill? I'd really like to take that down there before they close."

"Sure. Let me round up those little monkeys, and we'll meet you at the cabin."

"Great! I'm so lucky to have a best friend like you! See you in a few."

After delivering all the donations to the store, Canaan walked over to Candace and Sammi, "Hey, Mom. Would it be alright if I go to Jake's for a while tonight? He really wants me to come over and play his new video game with him. His mom already said it's fine with her."

"I don't know, son. Aren't you worn out from all this hard work? I know I could use a nap," Candace replied as she laughed and winked in Sammi's direction. "What do you think, Sammi?"

"Well, he did work awful hard. He's such a good helper, he deserves to have a little fun."

"Okay then. I'll drop you off at Jake's on the way home and pick you up around 9."

"9?" Canaan whined, "That's not enough time to beat the game. How about 10?"

"9:30 and no later."

"Okay. Thanks, Mom. Thanks, Sammi."

"Anytime, kiddo," Sammi replied. "I'm going to head back to the camp and get some much needed rest myself. I'll see you later, Can. Thanks for being such a wonderful best friend."

"My pleasure, Sam. See you later."

Chapter 14

Who could be knocking on my door at this time of the night? Sammi wondered as she checked the clock. 4:56. The alarm was set for 5:30. *Who could be here so early? And why?*

As she pulled herself out from under the twisted sheets, the knocking became pounding.

"Hold your horses! I'm coming!"

The sight she saw when she opened the door made her heart sink into her stomach. Jimmy was standing there, tear-stained face, trembling, with a look of shock still fresh in his eyes.

"Oh no! Jimmy! What's wrong?"

"Sa...Sa...Oh, God help me. Sammi, it's Candace..."

"Candace? What happened? Where is she?"

Tears filled Jimmy's eyes again and started falling quickly as he said, "Sh..she went to pick Canaan up from his friend Jake's house. When she wasn't home by eleven, I got worried. I called Jake's house, and his parents said she had left an hour earlier. That didn't seem right at all. I called the police and her car was found just off the road, down by the Mitchell's place. Th...there was an accident on their way back. The officers think a deer or something must have jumped in front of her. It looks like she swerved, lost control on the wet road, and went through a fence. Part of a fence post broke off and came through the windshield right into...right into..." Jimmy motioned with his hands to indicate the post had gone into Candance's chest. "Oh, Sammi! She's gone! Just like that. My whole life..." Jimmy buried his face in his hands as his shoulders shook with sobbing.

Sammi could not believe her best friend was dead. It had to be a mistake, and she would make sure they straightened it all out. However, right now, she knew Jimmy needed her to be strong and help him through this. As she gathered her thoughts, she grabbed Jimmy's arm and led him into the living room. She sat him down on the couch and went to get him a drink.

Handing him a glass of water, she realized what he had said. "You said that she had picked up Canaan and was on their way home? What about Canaan? Is he alright?"

"He's in shock, but the EMTs said he wasn't injured physically. Apparently, he had been so tired that he laid down in the back seat which is probably what kept him safe. But he will have to deal with waking up and seeing his mother with that fence post...Oh, Sammi! What a terrible thing for someone so young to have to witness! Why didn't I go get him and let her stay with Cady?" At this, Jimmy broke down into uncontrollable sobs.

Sammi couldn't do anything other than hold him and try to convince him that everything would be all right when she didn't believe it herself. "We'll get through this together...some how. We have to for the kids," she spoke hollowly, wondering as she did how in the world they would be able to survive, to enjoy life without Candace. She had always been there for Sammi, not to mention Jimmy and the kids. Now who could they depend upon?

As Jimmy wiped his eyes and tried to gather his own strength, he began to apologize, "I wanted to tell you right away, but not on the phone, and of course, I couldn't leave Canaan or Cady. The doctors gave Canaan some meds to help him calm down and get some sleep, but poor little Cady was bawling her eyes out, crying over and over, 'Mamma. Oh, Mamma, no!"

"Oh, Jimmy! Those sweet children! I know how they must be feeling," Sammi barely got the words out before her own tears began flowing again. *Breathe, Sammi. These three need you to help them be strong,* she told herself.

Jimmy continued to explain, "I had to wait for Angie to come over and stay with them. Thankfully by then Cady had fallen asleep as well, but Angie wanted to be sure I was alright before she would let me drive over here. She's a strong lady, but I can't imagine what this is like for her."

"Angie has always been tough, but we'll have to help her through this too. Why don't you get back to the house and try to get a little rest. I'll get dressed and come over in a while to help with breakfast and everything."

Not sure anyone would want to eat, Jimmy admitted that he did need to get home and that having her come over would be a big help with the kids. After he left, Sammi sank to the floor, with her back against the door, and the tears began to flow heavily once again. *Oh, Candace! It just can't be true! What will we do without you?*

The next few days were a blur. Sammi helped Jimmy with the funeral arrangements and the children. Canaan was more or less a zombie, understandably still in shock. The doctors gave him a prescription, but also recommended a psychiatrist, and Sammi made an appointment for the following Wednesday.

Every little reminder started the waterworks running down Cady's cheeks. Sammi was heartbroken for her. No one understood better than she did what it was like to go through life's greatest milestones without a mother, so Sammi determined that she would always be there for Cady and try her best to fill the gap.

Once again Dusty came back, heartbroken not only for the loss of his own friend, but more for the heartache that he knew Sammi must be going through, losing her best friend so shortly after her father's death.

"You just have way too much to handle alone right now. Let me stay for a week or two and help out."

"Dusty, I appreciate that, but you just got back to work. And there's Jimmy and the kids. I will be fine. I have to focus on them, not me. Besides, we can't both be missing so much work."

"I'm not leaving until after the funeral. Then I'll only go back to Cali for a day or two and finish smoothing out a couple of issues. Then I'll be back to help with everyone. You are a strong woman, but even you don't have enough strength for all you've been through lately."

It was a chilly November morning when they said their last goodbyes to Candace's body. Sammi and Jimmy agreed that Candace should be buried in the northwest corner of the campground on the family plot. As they gathered around the grave, the early morning sun shone on the dew making it sparkle like jewels.

How appropriate, Sammi thought. Candace was my greatest treasure, and now I'm placing her in the ground with all these gems shining around her. Oh, Candace, I can't believe I'll never see you again.

Just then, the preacher's words broke into Sammi's thoughts, "We know that Candace is in heaven now, and we will see her again someday."

There it is again. I guess everyone around here believes in all this religious stuff.

Brother Matt continued, "Jesus paid the price for our sins on the cross at Calvary. Anyone who believes and receives him as Savior has eternal life. When this life is over, we will join Him, and Candace, in heaven where we will spend all eternity without any pain or suffering. Candace loved Jesus, and I know she wants each of you to love Him too..."

Sammi felt a sudden uncomfortableness, but assumed it was due to all the stress of losing her best friend and worrying about Jimmy and the kids.

Mrs. Bakstrum approached the family after the service and offered her condolences. She hugged Jimmy, Canaan, and Cady, and then said a brief prayer that God would strengthen them through this difficult time. Jimmy thanked her and wiped a tear as he pulled his children closer to him. They would need each other's strength to get through this day and the days to follow.

Sammi gave Mrs. Bakstrum a hug and said, "Thank you so much for being here. I know it would have meant a lot to Candace." She wiped her eyes with a tissue and bit her lip to hold back more tears.

"Sammi, honey, I will always be here for you. If there's anything you need..."

"Thank you, Mrs. Bakstrum. I appreciate that so much."

"Why don't you come over for lunch one day next week. You still have my number, right? Just give me a call when you can."

"Okay, I'll try. Thanks again."

"I'll see you soon," Mrs. Bakstrum said as she walked away.

Chapter 15

The next Monday, Jimmy said he wanted to take Canaan and Cady to school and try to get some work done. Sammi agreed it could be good for all of them to get out of the house. She wanted to go get some groceries for them and maybe some holiday decorations to brighten up the house.

After shopping for a couple hours in the mall, she was desperately missing Candace. As teens, they had spent hours upon hours in that mall, shopping, eating, people watching, and just having fun together.

Maybe this wasn't such a good idea, she began to wonder. *I need to talk to somebody.*

Then she remembered her promise to Mrs. Bakstrum and gave her a call. Thirteen minutes later, she was being welcomed for lunch in Mrs. Bakstrum's home with the biggest hug the tiny lady could give.

"I'm afraid you'll have to settle for my second-place meal of lasagna today."

"Lasagna is my favorite, and I could really use some good comfort food."

"I figured as much, Sammi dear." Mrs. Bakstrum led Sammi into the kitchen and began dishing out lasagna onto their plates. Then she added some breadsticks, hot and fresh out of the oven.

"Yum! This is so good!" Sammi said with a mouthful. "Forgive my manners, but it's so delicious I don't want to stop eating long enough to tell you." Sammi laughed.

Mrs. Bakstrum smiled, "You're fine, dear. I'm just delighted to see you smile. I know the past couple of weeks have been extremely hard for you. I want you to know that I've been praying for you, Jimmy, Canaan, and Cady."

"Thank you. I know you loved Candace, too, and it probably hasn't been easy for you either."

"Death is never easy for anyone, but knowing I will see Candace again makes it just a little better. Also, knowing that she didn't suffer any in the accident, but went directly into the arms of Jesus makes it easier to accept, too."

"Mrs. Bakstrum, you know I've never bought into all this religious stuff, but it's starting to sound a lot nicer. I can hardly bear the thought that my very best friend in the world is gone, and I'll never see her again. If only I could hope to see her as you and so many others do..."

"Oh, but you can, Sammi. As long as you're still breathing, you still have a chance to accept Jesus' offer of forgiveness and salvation. Then you will join Jesus and Candace as well as your mom, dad and grandparents in heaven someday."

"I'm just not ready for that."

"Well, I'm not giving up on you."

"You know? Candace used to tell me the same thing, Mrs. Bakstrum."

"I know, dear. She loved you so much."

"Thank you. Thanks for this wonderful lunch too. I don't know how you do it. Dad tried to teach me to cook when I was little, but I never was much good at it."

"It just takes time, practice, and a little dab of love to make it taste even better." The two ladies laughed.

"I bet you could open a restaurant and name it 'Just a Dab of Love.' You could be rich and famous."

"Oh, honey, I'm too old for that. I've got a little spunk left but not near enough to be running a restaurant. I'll just keep making lunch for myself and a few close friends like you. That's what I consider you to be, you know?"

"Why, Mrs. Bakstrum, that is very nice of you. I consider you to be a good friend too."

"Then I believe it's time that you drop all this 'Mrs. Bakstrum' talk and start calling me Mary."

Sammi smiled as her heart lightened ever so slightly. "Thank you, Mary, for being my friend."

"You're quite welcome, and remember my door is always open. Maybe I'll even teach you to cook a little before it's over."

"That may take a miracle!"

"Well, I happen to know Someone who is in the miracle business, and I believe He still has great plans for you, when you're ready to accept Him."

"I'm not so sure about that."

"Oh, I am. You'll see. Just wait."

"This has really been nice. I needed this. Thank you again, Mrs...I mean, Mary, but I better be going. I need to pick up some groceries before Canaan and Cady get home."

"Anytime, sweetie, anytime."

Dusty managed to get a week off and came back on Thursday. Sammi opened the door to find him standing with sundae in hand and an enormous smile on his face. "Surprise!"

"Dusty! What? How?"

"Can't have my girl suffering withdrawals alone. Plus I thought you could use more support and help."

"Well, you do have my favorite dessert in your hand, so I guess I'm obligated to invite you in and help you eat that," Sammi said with a smile as she grabbed Dusty's arm and pulled him through the doorway. "I didn't expect to see you until Saturday, but thank goodness you're here early. As soon as I finished cleaning Dad's house, I started helping Jimmy with Candace's stuff. I don't know which of us has been crying more. That's not true; he has. It's so awful to see him in such pain. Every little thing is another painful memory for him. I shouldn't say painful. Some of the memories, or most of them, are wonderful, and they make him cry even more. The kids are struggling, too. I'm sorry to be dumping all this on you when you've barely walked in the door. Maybe you should hand over that sundae, so I'll stop talking."

"I figured that everyone would be having an extremely difficult time after losing someone as special as Candace. That's why I made sure I got back sooner rather than later. I don't have to be back in Cali until a week from Monday, so whatever I need to do to help, here I am," Dusty announced as he stretched his arms open wide.

Sammi took that opportunity to step in and wrap her arms around him. "Those may be the most wonderful words I've heard in a long, long time," she said as he closed his arms around her.

"We will get through this. Sammi, I really want you to think about closing this deal between you and me."

"Deal? What are you talking about?"

Dusty took a step back, knelt on one knee, and proposed, "Let's make it official. Sammi, will you marry me?" Then he quickly pulled a small, aqua bottle from his pocket. There was a cork in the mouth of the bottle and a bow of brown twine around the neck. Inside the bottle was just a tiny bit of sand and a beautiful, princess cut diamond ring.

"Oh! Dusty! This bottle reminds me of the one you gave me with the tiny beach house in it. How sweet that you... Well, of course you remembered!" Sammi said as tears formed in her eyes.

"That's right, but, don't you forget that I'm down on my knee here, waiting for an answer."

"Yes! I'd love to marry you. As long as we don't have to do it today, or even next week."

"Of course, the wedding will have to wait until things settle down. Now the toughest thing I have to ask you is..."

"What? You know you can ask me anything."

"I want you to move back here with me. I know your advertising means so much to you and how much you love the beach and California, but I have been thinking about Jimmy and the kids, and the camp, and well, he's really going to need our help."

"I have been thinking the same thing. I just don't know if I can yet. I don't know if I can *not* move back either. It's just so confusing dealing with all this."

"I understand that. For now, I'm just happy knowing you're my fiancé. Please consider the move back though, and let me know when the time is right. Deal?"

"Deal. Now, how in the world do you get this ring out of this bottle?"

"Very simply, my dear Brownie Lou. May I?" He asked as he rose from his knee and took the bottle from her hand. "You carefully unscrew the bottom." He retrieved the ring, placed it on her finger, and declared, "Even the most precious gem is nothing compared to you." Then he gently kissed her hand.

"Thank you, Dusty Fudge. I love you."

"Well, I certainly hope so. After all, you are

now the future Mrs. Dusty Fudge, and I love you too."

Chapter 16

Three weeks had passed since the funeral. Cady had just walked into Sammi's room, slumped down on the bed and was pouting.

"Why do you have to go now?" she complained.

Sammi's boss had been calling over and over for the past few days, and she knew she had to return to California to take care of business. She tried explaining it to Cady again.

"I know you got to work and have bills, but why can't you just keep working from here? Why do you have to go so far away when I still need you."

"Oh, sweet Cady girl, I think you will always need me; at least, I hope you do. I only have to go for a few days to meet with some new clients and present my proposals to them. These things have to be done face to face. I promise the week will fly by faster than you think, and I'll be back here with you."

"You promise you'll be back before Christmas?"

"I told you I would. I'll bring you some special presents from Cali too."

"I don't care about the gifts. I just want you. I

miss mama so much. I don't want you to leave me too."

"Cady, you know your mom didn't leave you on purpose. She loved you so much and wanted to always be here for you."

"I know. I know. I'm just having a hard time adjusting to her being gone. Brother Matt said I should be happy knowing that she is with Jesus, but I can't stop missing her. Some days I just want to go to heaven and hug her and never let go."

"Sweetie, please don't talk like that. I know how you feel. I miss your mom so much. But your dad still needs you here. Think how he would feel if he lost you too. I'm sure it would be worse than you feel about me leaving for less than a week."

"Oh my! You're right, Sammi. I'm so sorry. I didn't mean it that way."

"It's okay, Cady. We're all still hurting so much. We've got to be strong and help each other. No more crying about my trip to Cali now, alright?"

"Alright, but just make sure you hurry back."

"Deal. Now let me finish my packing, and then we'll order some pizza and have a family movie night."

"Pizza? Yes! I'll go tell Canaan and Dad."

"Okay, this shouldn't take me long. I'll be there in a little bit."

Cady ran out calling for Canaan to help her pick out a movie. Sammi could hear them arguing over which movie to watch as she looked around to be sure she had packed everything she needed. That's when she saw it; Candace's Bible lay on the desk. Sammi felt drawn to it; she didn't understand why. As she picked it up, she noticed a faded sheet of paper sticking out of it. She pulled it out and began to read. It was Candace's prayer list, and there was Sammi's name at the top of the list. Sammi's eyes filled with tears as she remembered Candace telling her that she would never stop praying for her to accept Jesus.

I don't think Candace would mind if I borrow this, she thought as she gently placed the Bible in her bag. After zipping up the bag, Sammi turned off the lights and went to the kitchen to order the pizza.

The family movie night was a success after they decided to watch both of the movies that Canaan and Cady had chosen. Early the next morning, Jimmy, Canaan, and Cady tearfully said their good-byes to Sammi and wished her a safe, and quick, trip.

Chapter 17

Sammi's flight landed in time for her to attend the Christmas Eve service with Jimmy and the kids. Since she left, she'd been reading the book of John in Candace's Bible, and as she listened to the songs and performers sharing the meaning of Christmas and the importance of Christ's birth as it related to His sacrifice on the cross, she remembered all the times her father had read the nativity story on Christmas Eve. She felt an uneasiness in her stomach. She wasn't sure why, but she couldn't shake the feeling.

When they returned to the house, Sammi excused herself to her room, claiming that her head was hurting. *How could she explain to them that the service left her feeling confused and somewhat ashamed?*

"Dad, do you think Sammi is alright?" Cady asked. "She was so quiet after church."

"I think she may be under some conviction. With all the changes in her life this past year, I believe God is softening her heart toward Him. We need to keep praying that she will answer His call."

"You really think so? Oh, that would be so awesome!" Cady squealed with glee. "I'm going to go to my prayer closet right now!"

"Great idea, sweetie." Jimmy said his own prayer for Sammi as Cady raced out of the kitchen. Canaan was nearly knocked over by Cady as he entered the room.

"Whoa! Where's the fire? What's got into Cady?"

"She's going to pray for Sammi. We think she may be almost ready to give her heart to Jesus."

"Cool! I sure hope so!" Canaan grabbed a couple of cookies from the cookie jar on the counter. "I'm going to go pray for her too, then. She won't have a choice with all of us praying for her."

In her room, Sammi was trying hard to figure out what was going on with her. *I've never felt this confused about this religious stuff. Why now?* She noticed Candace's Bible sticking out of her bag, picked it up, opened it, and began reading.

"For God so loved the world that He gave His only begotten Son, that whosoever believeth in Him should not perish but have everlasting life."

The preacher mentioned this during the service. How odd that I should open to this verse. What was it the preacher said? Oh yeah...'you have to believe that Jesus was God's Son, that He lived a perfect life, and gave His life on the cross to pay the price for your sins.' If I don't, I will go hell when I die, but if I do believe, I will go to heaven. I just don't know.

"Oh, Can, I miss you. I wish you were here to help me understand this."

There was a knock on her bedroom door, and Cady stuck her head in the room. "Sammi, may I come in?"

Sammi sat the Bible on the nightstand and replied, "Sure, honey. What's up?"

"I was just worried about you. You were awful quiet after church. How's your head?"

"Well, honestly, Cady, it wasn't my head. Not really. I was just feeling so confused about all this. I still am. I really wish your mom was here to explain some things to me. I sure could use her help."

"What is confusing you? Maybe I can help explain it."

"It just seems too easy. I must be missing something. And how do I know for sure that this Jesus bringing salvation from sins stuff is real?"

"The Bible says it's true, so I believe it. I realize people like to have better proof, but I can only tell you what Jesus has done in my life." Cady shared her experience of accepting Jesus and how He made a difference in her life, especially helping her through the last month after her mother's accident. She showed Sammi different verses in the Bible that explain how Jesus said He would never leave us, that He sent the Holy Spirit to bear witness with our spirits and to assure us that we belong to God and will live with Him forever. "His Spirit comforts us in tough times and convicts us when we sin. That's why I believe it's true."

"Cady, you are so wise for such a young lady. You have really helped explain this to me, and I think I would like to accept Jesus as my Savior. I'm just not sure how to do that."

"I'd be happy to help you with that too," Cady said with the biggest smile ever. She led Sammi in a simple prayer, confessing that she was a sinner in need of saving and that she believed Jesus died, was buried, and raised again the third day to be the Savior she needs, and asking Him to live in her heart and help her to live for Him.

After saying the prayer, both wiped tears from their eyes. Then Cady grabbed Sammi in a bear hug that almost never ended. "Oh my goodness! I can't believe it! Thank You, Jesus, for saving Sammi. Help her to know You are real and to follow You. Oh, Sammi! You did it! You're going to be in heaven with us! I'm so happy! This is the BEST Christmas gift since the birth of Jesus Himself! Praise the Lord!" Cady squealed with excitement.

"I already feel different. Is that how it always works?"

"Yep."

"Thank you, Cady. I'm so glad you came to my room tonight. Now what do I do?"

"We've got to tell Dad and Canaan! Come on! They've been praying for you, too. That's what I was doing, and I just felt like God wanted me to come and talk to you, help you. He works that way sometimes. He's pretty awesome. You'll see as you read your Bible and get to know Him better. Come on! We got to tell...DAD! CANAAN! Come quick!"

Both guys came running asking what was wrong.

"Nothing is wrong. Tell them, Sammi!"

"I was feeling confused, and after Cady explained some things to me...well, I prayed to accept Jesus as my Savior."

"Hallelujah! That's wonderful!" Jimmy whooped, embracing Sammi.

"Praise the Lord! Our prayers have been answered!" Canaan exclaimed.

Jimmy added, "This calls for a celebration! Let's all go into the kitchen and have some cookies and ice cream!"

"I just wish Mom was here. She prayed for you for so many years. She would be happier than the three of us put together," Canaan sighed.

"I guess we'll have to wait to celebrate with her when we get to heaven," Sammi suggested.

"Oh, I'm sure that she's celebrating with us tonight," Jimmy stated. "The Bible says the heavens rejoice when a sinner accepts Jesus. I bet your dad is celebrating too."

"Don't forget about my mom. Oh, and my dad! Can you imagine how happy he is now?" Sammi exclaimed as tears of joy began to fill her eyes again.

The four went into the kitchen and laughed and talked for over an hour. Jimmy and the kids chiming in to answer questions Sammi had as they celebrated her new birth as a Christian.

Cady gasped and asked, "You know who else should be celebrating? If only you would let him know what's happened..."

"Oh my goodness! Dusty! I've got to call him! Excuse me, guys!" Sammi yelled as she ran for her phone. The other three laughed, smiling at each other.

"Praise the Lord! Sammi, you've just made my whole year so much more wonderful! You know how much I want to marry you, but I've been struggling with it because I can't go against my personal convictions. The Bible teaches us not to be unequally yoked, you know? Now, God has answered that prayer. It just shows you that when we step out of His way, He will take care of all the details. I can't wait to make you my heaven-sent bride."

"Before I can be your bride, I need to be honest with you. I've come to realize something about myself, Dusty," Sammi began. "I realize I was the problem in our relationship before. You always tried so hard to make things right for me, but I wouldn't listen. When you started talking about your God and how you became a Christian, I would shut you out. I didn't want any part of that life."

"Sammi, I only wanted you to experience the joy I found in Jesus."

"I realize that now. I've been searching for answers for so long, and I never knew it. All the time I've spent out here at Camp Green Forest lately has given me a lot of time to think. I can't believe the place is in such a mess. I wish I had come home sooner. I should have come home before my father passed away." Tears began to fill Sammi's eyes, but she did not want to cry. Not now. This is supposed to be a happy time. "Helping Jimmy with the kids over the past month has changed me somehow. I'm not sure how I can leave here now. I'm going to talk to Bob about my position at the agency after the holidays are over."

"Are you sure, Sammi? You love your job."

"I'm positive. I love this place even more than... if you don't mind me using our saying this way, but more than brownie loves fudge."

"It's perfect! I've been praying for that too. Camp Green Forest has always meant so much to me, and now that Jimmy needs help fixing it and running it, I've been looking for a way to move back there. Mom is going to be so happy!"

"I guess we are totally on the same page now, both geographically and spiritually. All that's left is a wedding. When did you have in mind, Dusty?"

"What do you say to a quaint little ceremony at the campground next month?"

"I'd say...I think we've seen that there are no guarantees about tomorrow. Can we make it a New Year's ceremony?"

"Oh, Brownie Lou, I love you more than fudge, you know. I'll make arrangements and be there this weekend. We'll make a trip over to Mom's to tell her all the good news. Then we'll get all the details worked out."

"Sounds great. See you then, Dusty Fudge. I love

you, too."

Mrs. Bakstrum was delighted when Sammi called and asked if she could come over for lunch again. She could tell Sammi was excited, but Sammi said she had to tell her why face to face. When she opened the door, Sammi was beaming with a smile so large it barely fit through the doorway. Mrs. Bakstrum knew right away that Sammi had given her heart to Jesus.

"God is so good! You don't have to say a word. I know you've finally accepted Jesus! Praise the Lord for answered prayers!" Mrs. Bakstrum proclaimed.

"Wow! I didn't know it would be so evident, but there's more."

"Well, come on in and tell me all about it. Come, come."

Sammi followed Mrs. Bakstrum into the kitchen and shared how she had been reading Candace's Bible and had gotten so confused, how Cady, Canaan, and Jimmy had been praying for her, how Cady had come into her room and explained it all, and how they had prayed together. Then she began to tell her about sharing the news with Dusty and how he had been praying as well. She told her all about the wedding plans and the decision to move back and help Jimmy run the camp.

Mrs. Bakstrum was almost as excited as Sammi was. "Darling, that is so wonderful! God is working in mighty ways! I'm so blessed to get to share in all this with you."

"More blessed than you know. Mrs. Bakstrum...I mean, Mary...I'd be honored if you would be a part of our wedding ceremony. With Candace being gone, I'd love for my new best friend to be my maid of honor."

"You mean me? Why, of course, I'd be delighted! What a way to begin the New Year!"

The two made a list of all that needed to be done before the first. Then Mary called Brother Matt to come over for a visit. The two ladies told him about Sammi's conversion and the wedding plans. He agreed to perform the ceremony for them, and they discussed Sammi's wishes for the arrangements. After everything was settled, Sammi thanked Brother Matt and Mary and then excused herself.

"I'd better get over to Jimmy's and let him and the kids know about all this. They'll definitely be more excited than we are. Especially Cady. She did NOT want me to go back to California. She's probably going to jump for joy straight through the roof."

Mary laughed, "No doubt about that. They are extremely blessed to have friends like you and Dusty. See you soon, dear."

Chapter 18

New Year's Day was a beautiful sunlit day, and the small group gathered in the clearing next to the family burial plot. It's not everyday that a bride requests the ceremony be held next to a graveyard, but Sammi thought it only appropriate to include her parents and her best friend Candace. She knew they were not really there in that cold, hard ground, but she felt closer to them, like their spirits were somehow surrounding her.

Sammi had come to the graveyard early to apologize to her father for not coming home before he passed and to share with him all that had happened. She prayed that he had forgiven her and believed he had, just as Candace had told her. Between the headstones, Sammi made a vow to never take a single day for granted, but to enjoy every moment with her friends and family.

Now as Canaan began to play the wedding march from his iPod, Jimmy led Sammi down the makeshift aisle where he gave her away and took his place as the best man next to Dusty. Mary Bakstrum couldn't help but cry tears of joy as she watched her prayers being answered as her young friend became Mrs. Dusty Newall.

Dusty couldn't believe he was finally standing there with the love of his life, finally becoming her husband, knowing that she had given her life to Jesus and they would be leading many teens to the Lord each summer at the camp. It was overwhelmingly amazing. He looked up at the sky with a smile and thanked the Lord again for answering his prayers above and beyond his wildest dreams.

Hannah Newall stood nearby with the two kids, making the wedding party complete. She was excited for Dusty and Sammi, almost as excited as she was for herself. She was finally getting the daughter-in-law she had longed for for so many years. She had loved Sammi from that first year she had worked at the camp. She had often prayed for this day, and now God was answering her prayers. She also thanked God for answering in His time.

Jimmy, Canaan, and Cady each thanked God for answering their prayers as well, but no one had as much to be thankful for as Sammi did. She thanked God for giving her chance after chance, for the great friends He had given her who had never given up on her, for the family legacy that finally had gotten through to her, for Dusty and his love for her, for Jimmy and the kids, and for the years she had with her dad and Candace. Her heart overflowed with the love she had been given. She knew she was extremely blessed, and she couldn't wait to begin her new life with Dusty as co-owners of Camp Green

Forest with Jimmy and the kids.

"I do," she said.

"Then by the powers vested in me..."

After the kiss, Sammi turned around and was surprised to see Harvey and Marlena. "Oh my goodness! Harvey! Marlena! When did you two get here?"

"Just before the preacher asked if anyone knew of any reason that you two shouldn't be married. Marlena was about to say something, but I stopped her. You're welcome," Harvey winked at Sammi as Marlena elbowed him in the gut.

"Always such a kidder, aren't you? Anyway, I'm so glad you made it!"

"We couldn't miss our daughter's wedding," Marlena exclaimed, taking the bride into her arms for a giant hug. Then she turned to Dusty and hugged him tight. "Welcome to the family, son. We're so happy for the both of you." Turning around, she said, "You must be Jimmy, Canaan and Cady. We've heard so much about you. It's nice to finally meet you."

Jimmy and the kids looked lost. Sammi spoke up, "Harvey and Marlena kind of adopted me since I had no family in California. I've told you about them before."

"Yes, I remember. I just never expected to see them today. Especially way out here."

Dusty stepped over and put his arm around his new bride. "Well, I couldn't allow my Sammi to get married without the nearest thing she has to parents. I called in a favor and they agreed to come surprise her. Harvey agreed that you should still give her away though, Jimmy."

"Oh, Dusty. Thank you so much! Aren't I the luckiest bride ever?" Sammi questioned.

Cady squealed with delight, "Just when I thought the day couldn't be more perfect for you. Great call, Dusty!"   "Thanks," Dusty said quietly. "Anything for my Sammi. I love you."

"And I love you."

"Okay, don't start the mushy stuff again. Isn't it time for some cake?" Canaan asked.

"Yes, the cake. Everyone back to the cabin," Jimmy led the group to the house for refreshments.

As the festivities were coming to an end, Harvey and Marlena revealed that they planned to stay and help Jimmy and the kids until Dusty and Sammi took care of things in California after their honeymoon and got back and settled in at Camp Green Forest.

"Are you sure you can stay that long?"

"Of course, Sammi. Don't worry about a thing. We've got it covered," Harvey declared.

"Yea! Hey, Canaan, it looks like we've got some grandparents for a few weeks!" Cady exclaimed.

Marlena was just as excited. "Harvey, we've got grandkids now too! How much more blessed could we be?"

Harvey smiled as the two kids grabbed him and Marlena in a group hug.

Dusty's mom broke in, "Hey, don't forget about this grandma. What a terrific day!"

Everyone laughed. Then Brother Matt said a prayer of blessing and thanksgiving for the abundance of love before leaving the celebration.

Chapter 19

Sitting on a bench beneath an old pine tree in the family graveyard, Sammi spoke to her best friend. "Candace, I wish you were still here to help us all. You would be so pleased with everything we've done. Jimmy maintains the campgrounds, Dusty keeps the books, and I create the advertising flyers and website. We even got Canaan to help us with the technical and computer stuff as well as the sound and projections during the nightly sermons. Cady is helping Dusty's mom run the kitchen this year too. It's become a real family run camp again. I feel like Mom and Dad would be happy.

"You were right when you said God works in mysterious ways. All my life I was running from religion. Now I wish I hadn't. When Dusty came back into my life, I started to see that I needed God, but I was still running. Then after Dad passed and you had your accident, I found your Bible and started reading. I finally realized my need for Jesus and accepted Him. It seems like my life changed so quickly after that.

"Now I wish that I would have listened to you and Dad years ago. I thought I was living the good life, running around the world and having fun, but it doesn't even compare with the good life I'm living now. Or the good life I'll get to live with you all in heaven when I die. I can never thank you enough for always praying for me and never giving up on me. You truly were my best friend. I miss you so much! I'll see you again someday, my friend. I love you."

Placing a bouquet of flowers on Candace's grave, Sammi smiled, wiped a tear of joy from her right eye, and turned to walk back to the camp's tabernacle for the evening service. As she neared the open-sided building, she could hear the voices of the nearly two hundred fifty campers and counselors singing, "I have decided to follow Jesus." Sammi turned her face to the sky and joined in the song, "No turning back. No turning back."

Made in USA - Crawfordsville, IN
41917_9798634331621
05.04.2020 0652